"Give Me the Box!"

One night when he was lying in his bed, Michael heard a voice.

"Give me the box," it said.

Michael sat up.

"Who are you?" he asked.

"I am the angel," said the voice. "I have come for my box."

"You are not my angel," shouted Michael. He was beginning to grow frightened.

"Your angel has sent me. Give me the box."

"No. I can only give it to my angel."

"Give me the box!"

"No!" cried Michael.

There was a roar, and a rumble of thunder. A cold wind came shrieking through his bedroom. . . .

Books by Bruce Coville

Chamber of Horrors
  Amulet of Doom
  Spirits and Spells
  Eyes of the Tarot
  Waiting Spirits

The A.I. Gang Trilogy
  Operation Sherlock
  Robot Trouble
  Forever Begins Tomorrow

Bruce Coville's Alien
Adventures
  Aliens Ate My Homework
  I Left My Sneakers in
    Dimension X
  The Search for Snout

Camp Haunted Hills
  How I Survived My
    Summer Vacation
  Some of My Best Friends
    Are Monsters
  The Dinosaur that
    Followed Me Home

Magic Shop Books
  Jennifer Murdley's Toad
  Jeremy Thatcher, Dragon
    Hatcher
  The Monster's Ring

My Teacher Books
  My Teacher Is an Alien
  My Teacher Fried My Brains
  My Teacher Glows in the Dark
  My Teacher Flunked the Planet

Space Brat Books
  Space Brat
  Space Brat 2: Blork's Evil Twin
  Space Brat 3: The Wrath of
    Squat
  Space Brat 4: Planet of the Dips

  The Dragonslayers
  Goblins in the Castle
  Monster of the Year
  The World's Worst Fairy
    Godmother

Available from MINSTREL Books

Bruce Coville

Oddly Enough

AN ARCHWAY PAPERBACK
Published by POCKET BOOKS
New York London Toronto Sydney Tokyo Singapore

An Archway Paperback published by
POCKET BOOKS, a division of Simon & Schuster Inc.
1230 Avenue of the Americas, New York, NY 10020

Copyright © 1994 by Bruce Coville
Illustrations copyright © 1994 by Michael Hussar

Published by arrangement with Harcourt Brace, Inc.

ISBN: 0-671-51693-0

First Archway Paperback printing January 1997

10 9 8 7 6 5 4 3 2 1

AN ARCHWAY PAPERBACK and colophon are registered trademarks of Simon & Schuster Inc.

Cover art by Gennady Spirin

Printed in the U.S.A.

IL 6+

For Helen Buckley Simkewicz,

who told me I could write when it was the thing I needed most in the world to hear. Many thanks.

Contents

The Box

ONCE THERE was a boy who had a box.

The boy's name was Michael, and the box was very special because it had been given to him by an angel.

Michael knew it had been an angel because of the huge white wings he wore. So he took very good care of the box, because the angel had asked him to.

And he never, ever opened it.

When Michael's mother asked him where he had gotten the box, he said, "an angel gave it to me."

"That's nice, dear," she answered, and went back to stirring her cake mix.

Michael carried the box with him wherever he went. He took it to school. He took it out to play. He set it by his place at mealtimes.

After all, he never knew when the angel would come back and ask for it.

The box was very beautiful. It was made of dark wood and carved with strange designs. The carvings were smooth and polished, and they seemed to glow whenever they caught the light. A pair of tiny golden hinges, and a miniature golden latch that Michael never touched, held the cover tight to the body of the box.

Michael loved the way it felt against his fingers.

Sometimes Michael's friends would tease him about the box.

"Hey, Michael," they would say. "How come you never come out to play without that box?"

"Because I am taking care of it for an angel," he would answer. And because this was true, the boys would leave him alone.

At night, before he went to bed, Michael would rub the box with a soft cloth to make it smooth and glossy.

Sometimes when he did this he could hear something moving inside the box.

He wondered how it was that something could stay alive in the box without any food or water.

But he did not open the box. The angel had asked him not to.

One night when he was lying in his bed, Michael heard a voice.

"Give me the box," it said.

Michael sat up.

"Who are you?" he asked.

"I am the angel," said the voice. "I have come for my box."

"You are not my angel," shouted Michael. He was beginning to grow frightened.

"Your angel has sent me. Give me the box."

"No. I can only give it to my angel."

"Give me the box!"

"No!" cried Michael.

There was a roar, and a rumble of thunder. A cold wind came shrieking through his bedroom.

"I must have that box!" sobbed the voice, as though its heart was breaking.

"No! No!" cried Michael, and he clutched the box tightly to his chest.

But the voice was gone.

Soon Michael's mother came in to comfort him, telling him he must have had a bad dream. After a time he stopped crying and went back to sleep.

But he knew the voice had been no dream.

After that night Michael was twice as careful with the box as he had been before. He grew to love it deeply. It reminded him of his angel.

* * *

As Michael grew older the box became more of a problem for him.

His teachers began to object to him keeping it constantly at his side or on his desk. One particularly thick and unbending teacher even sent him to the principal. But when Michael told the principal he was taking care of the box for an angel, the principal told Mrs. Jenkins to leave him alone.

When Michael entered junior high he found that the other boys no longer believed him when he told them why he carried the box. He understood that. They had never seen the angel, as he had. Most of the children were so used to the box by now that they ignored it anyway.

But some of the boys began to tease Michael about it.

One day two boys grabbed the box and began a game of keep-away with it, throwing it back and forth above Michael's head, until one of them dropped it.

It landed with an ugly smack against the concrete.

Michael raced to the box and picked it up. One of the fine corners was smashed flat, and a piece of one of the carvings had broken off.

"I hate you," he started to scream. But the words choked in his throat, and the hate died within him.

He picked up the box and carried it home. Then he cried for a little while.

The boys were very sorry for what they had done. But they never spoke to Michael after that, and secretly they hated him, because they had done something so mean to him, and he had not gotten mad.

For seven nights after the box was dropped Michael did not hear any noise inside it when he was cleaning it.

He was terrified.

What if everything was ruined? What could he tell the angel? He couldn't eat or sleep. He refused to go to school. He simply sat beside the box, loving it and caring for it.

On the eighth day he could hear the movements begin once more, louder and stronger than ever.

He sighed, and slept for eighteen hours.

When he entered high school Michael did not go out for sports, because he was not willing to leave the box alone. He certainly could not take it out onto a football field with him.

He began taking art classes instead. He wanted to learn to paint the face of his angel. He tried over and over again, but he could never get the pictures to come out the way he wanted them to.

Everyone else thought they were beautiful.

But they never satisfied Michael.

Whenever Michael went out with a girl she would ask him what he had in the box. When he told her he didn't know, she would not believe him. So then he would tell her the story of how the angel had given him the box. Then the girl would think he was fooling her. Sometimes a girl would try to open the box when he wasn't looking.

But Michael always knew, and whenever a girl did this, he would never ask her out again.

Finally Michael found a girl who believed him. When he told her that an angel had given him the box, and that he had to take care of it for him, she nodded her head as if this was the most sensible thing she had ever heard.

Michael showed her the pictures he had painted of his angel.

They fell in love, and after a time they were married.

Things were not so hard for Michael now, because he had someone who loved him to share his problems with.

But it was still not easy to care for the box. When he tried to get a job people would ask him why he carried it, and usually they would laugh at him. More than once he was fired from his work because his boss would get sick of seeing the box and not being able to find out what was in it.

Finally Michael found work as a night custodian. He carried the box in a little knapsack on his back, and did his job so well that no one ever questioned him.

One night Michael was driving to work. It was raining, and very slippery. A car turned in front of him. There was an accident, and both Michael and the box flew out of the car.

When Michael woke up he was in the hospital. The first thing he asked for was his box. But it was not there.

Michael jumped out of bed, and it took three nurses and two doctors to wrestle him back into it. They gave him a shot to make him sleep.

That night, when the hospital was quiet, Michael snuck out of bed and got his clothes.

It was a long way to where he had had the accident, and he had to walk the whole distance. He searched for hours under the light of a bright, full moon, until finally he found the box. It was caked with mud, and another of the beautiful corners had been flattened in. But none of the carvings were broken, and when he held it to his ear, he could hear something moving inside.

When the nurse came to check him in the morning, she found Michael sleeping peacefully, with a dirty box beside him on the bed. She reached out to take it, but his hand wrapped around the box and held it in a grip of steel. He did not even wake up.

Michael would have had a hard time paying the hospital bills. But one day a man came to their house and saw some of his paintings. He asked if he could buy one. Other people heard about them, and before long Michael was selling many paintings. He quit his night job, and began to make his living as an artist.

But he was never able to paint a picture of the angel that looked the way it should.

One night when Michael was almost thirty he heard the voice again.

"Give me the box!" it cried, in tones so strong and stern that Michael was afraid he would obey them.

But he closed his eyes, and in his mind he saw his angel again, with his face so strong and his eyes so full of love, and he paid no attention to the voice at all.

The next morning Michael went to his easel and began to paint. It was the most beautiful picture he had ever made.

But still it did not satisfy him.

The voice came after Michael seven times that

year, but he was never tempted to answer it again.

Michael and his wife had two children, and they loved them very much. The children were always curious about the box their father carried, and one day, when Michael was napping, the oldest child tried to open it.

Michael woke and saw what was happening. For the first time in his memory he lost his temper.

He raised his hand to strike his son.

But in the face of his child he suddenly saw the face of the angel he had met only once, so long ago, and the anger died within him.

After that day the children left the box alone.

Time went on. The children grew up and went to their own homes. Michael and his wife grew old. The box suffered another accident or two. It was battered now, and even the careful polishing Michael gave it every night did not hide the fact that the carvings were growing thin from the pressure of his hands against them so many hours a day.

Once, when they were very old, Michael's wife said to him, "Do you really think the angel will come back for his box?"

"Hush, my darling," said Michael, putting his finger against her lips.

And she never knew if Michael believed the angel would come back or not.

After a time she grew sick, and died, and Michael was left alone.

Everybody in his town knew who he was, and when he could not hear they called him Crazy Michael, and whirled their fingers around their ears, and whispered that he had carried that box from the time he was eight years old.

Of course nobody really believed such a silly story.

But they all knew Michael was crazy.

Even so, in their hearts they wished they had a secret as enduring as the one that Crazy Michael carried.

One night, when Michael was almost ninety years old, the angel returned to him and asked for the box.

"Is it really you?" cried Michael. He struggled to his elbows to squint at the face above him. Then he could see that it was indeed the angel, who had not changed a bit in eighty years, while he had grown so old.

"At last," he said softly. "Where have you been all this time, Angel?"

"I have been working," said the angel. "And waiting." He knelt by Michael's bed. "Have you been faithful?"

"I have," whispered Michael.

"Give me the box, please."

Under the pillow, beside his head, the battered box lay waiting. Michael pulled it out and extended it to the angel.

"It is not as beautiful as when you first gave it to me," he said, lowering his head.

"That does not matter," said the angel.

He took the box from Michael's hands. Holding it carefully, he stared at it, as if he could see what was inside. Then he smiled.

"It is almost ready."

Michael smiled, too. "What is it?" he asked. His face seemed to glow with happiness. "Tell me what it is at last."

"I cannot," whispered the angel sadly.

Michael's smile crumpled. "Then tell me this," he said after a moment. "Is it important?" His voice was desperate.

"It will change the world," replied the angel.

Michael leaned back against his pillow. "Then surely I will know what it is when this has come to pass," he said, smiling once again.

"No. You will not know," answered the angel.

"But if it is so important that it will change the world, then . . ."

"*You* have changed the world, Michael. How many people know that?"

The angel shimmered and began to disappear.

Michael stretched out his hand. "Wait!" he cried.

The angel reached down. He took Michael's withered hand and held it tightly in his own.

"You have done well," he whispered.

He kissed Michael softly on the forehead.

And then he was gone.

Duffy's Jacket

F MY COUSIN Duffy had the brains of a turnip it never would have happened. But as far as I'm concerned, Duffy makes a turnip look bright. My mother disagrees. According to her, Duffy is actually very bright. She claims the reason he's so scatterbrained is that he's too busy being brilliant inside his own head to remember everyday things. Maybe. But hanging around with Duffy means you spend a lot of time saying, "Your glasses, Duffy," or "Your coat, Duffy," or—well, you get the idea: a lot of three-word sentences that start with "Your," end with

"Duffy," and have words like *book, radio, wallet,* or whatever it is he's just put down and left behind, stuck in the middle.

Me, I think turnips are brighter.

But since Duffy's my cousin, and since my mother and her sister are both single parents, we tend to do a lot of things together—like camping, which is how we got into the mess I want to tell you about.

Personally, I thought camping was a big mistake. But since Mom and Aunt Elise are raising the three of us—me, Duffy, and my little sister, Marie—on their own, they're convinced they have to do man-stuff with us every once in a while. I think they read some book that said me and Duffy would come out weird if they don't. You can take him camping all you want. It ain't gonna make Duffy normal.

Anyway, the fact that our mothers were getting wound up to do something fatherly, combined with the fact that Aunt Elise's boss had a friend who had a friend who said we could use his cabin, added up to the five of us bouncing along this horrible dirt road late one Friday in October.

It was late because we had lost an hour going back to get Duffy's suitcase. I suppose it wasn't actually Duffy's fault. No one remembered to say, "Your suitcase, Duffy," so he couldn't really have been expected to remember it.

"Oh, Elise," cried my mother, as we got deeper into the woods. "Aren't the leaves beautiful?"

That's why it doesn't make sense for them to try to do man-stuff with us. If it had been our fathers, they would have been drinking beer and burping and maybe telling dirty stories instead of talking about the leaves. So why try to fake it?

Anyway, we get to this cabin, which is about eighteen million miles from nowhere, and to my surprise, it's not a cabin at all. It's a house. A big house.

"Oh, my," said my mother as we pulled into the driveway.

"Isn't it great?" chirped Aunt Elise. "It's almost a hundred years old, back from the time when they used to build big hunting lodges up here. It's the only one in the area still standing. Horace said he hasn't been able to get up here in some time. That's why he was glad to let us use it. He said it would be good to have someone go in and air the place out."

Leave it to Aunt Elise. This place didn't need airing out—it needed fumigating. I never saw so many spiderwebs in my life. From the sounds we heard coming from the walls, the mice seemed to have made it a population center. We found a total of two working lightbulbs: one in the kitchen, and one in the dining room, which was paneled with dark wood and had a big stone fireplace at one end.

"Oh, my," said my mother again.

Duffy, who's allergic to about fifteen different things, started to sneeze.

"Isn't it charming?" asked Aunt Elise hopefully.

No one answered her.

Four hours later we had managed to get three bedrooms clean enough to sleep in without getting the heebie-jeebies—one for Mom and Aunt Elise, one for Marie, and one for me and Duffy. After a supper of beans and franks we hit the hay, which I think is what our mattresses were stuffed with. As I was drifting off, which took about thirty seconds, it occurred to me that four hours of housework wasn't all that much of a man-thing, something it might be useful to remember the next time Mom got one of these plans into her head.

Things looked better in the morning when we went outside and found a stream where we could go wading. ("Your sneakers, Duffy.")

Later we went back and started poking around the house, which really was enormous.

That was when things started getting a little spooky. In the room next to ours I found a message scrawled on the wall. BEWARE THE SENTINEL, it said in big black letters.

When I showed Mom and Aunt Elise they said it was just a joke and got mad at me for frightening Marie.

Marie wasn't the only one who was frightened.

We decided to go out for another walk. ("Your lunch, Duffy.") We went deep into the woods, following a faint trail that kept threatening to disappear but never actually faded away altogether. It was a hot day, even in the deep woods, and after a while we decided to take off our coats.

When we got back and Duffy didn't have his jacket, did they get mad at him? My mother actually had the nerve to say, "Why didn't you remind him? You know he forgets things like that."

What do I look like, a walking memo pad?

Anyway, I had other things on my mind—like the fact that I was convinced someone had been following us while we were in the woods.

I tried to tell my mother about it, but first she said I was being ridiculous, and then she accused me of trying to sabotage the trip.

So I shut up. But I was pretty nervous, especially when Mom and Aunt Elise announced that they were going into town—which was twenty miles away—to pick up some supplies (like light-bulbs).

"You kids will be fine on your own," said Mom cheerfully. "You can make popcorn and play Monopoly. And there's enough soda here for you to make yourselves sick on."

And with that they were gone.

It got dark.

We played Monopoly.

They didn't come back. That didn't surprise me. Since Duffy and I were both fifteen they felt it was okay to leave us on our own, and Mom had warned us they might decide to have dinner at the little inn we had seen on the way up.

But I would have been happier if they had been there.

Especially when something started scratching on the door.

"What was that?" said Marie.

"What was what?" asked Duffy.

"That!" she said, and this time I heard it, too. My stomach rolled over, and the skin at the back of my neck started to prickle.

"Maybe it's the Sentinel!" I hissed.

"Andrew!" yelled Marie. "Mom told you not to say that."

"She said not to try to scare you," I said. "I'm not. *I'm* scared! I told you I heard something following us in the woods today."

Scratch, scratch.

"But you said it stopped," said Duffy. "So how would it know where we are now?"

"I don't know. I don't know what it is. Maybe it tracked us, like a bloodhound."

Scratch, scratch.

"Don't bloodhounds have to have something to give them a scent?" asked Marie. "Like a piece of clothing, or—"

We both looked at Duffy.

"Your jacket, Duffy!"

Duffy turned white.

"That's silly," he said after a moment.

"There's something at the door," I said frantically. "Maybe it's been lurking around all day, waiting for our mothers to leave. Maybe it's been waiting for years for someone to come back here."

Scratch, scratch.

"I don't believe it," said Duffy. "It's just the wind moving a branch. I'll prove it."

He got up and headed for the door. But he didn't open it. Instead he peeked through the window next to it. When he turned back, his eyes looked as big as the hard-boiled eggs we had eaten for supper.

"There's something out there!" he hissed. *"Something big!"*

"I told you," I cried. "Oh, I knew there was something there."

"Andrew, are you doing this just to scare me?" said Marie. "Because if you are—"

Scratch, scratch.

"Come on," I said, grabbing her by the hand. "Let's get out of here."

I started to lead her up the stairs.

"Not there!" said Duffy. "If we go up there, we'll be trapped."

"You're right," I said. "Let's go out the back way!"

The thought of going outside scared the daylights out of me. But at least out there we would have somewhere to run. Inside—well, who knew what might happen if the thing found us inside.

We went into the kitchen.

I heard the front door open.

"Let's get out of here!" I hissed.

We scooted out the back door. "What now?" I wondered, looking around frantically.

"The barn," whispered Duffy. "We can hide in the barn."

"Good idea," I said. Holding Marie by the hand, I led the way to the barn. But the door was held shut by a huge padlock.

The wind was blowing harder, but not hard enough to hide the sound of the back door of the house opening, and then slamming shut.

"Quick!" I whispered. "It knows we're out here. Let's sneak around front. It will never expect us to go back into the house."

Duffy and Marie followed me as I led them behind a hedge. I caught a glimpse of something heading toward the barn and swallowed nervously. It was big. Very big.

"I'm scared," whispered Marie.

"Shhh!" I hissed. "We can't let it know where we are."

We slipped through the front door. We locked it, just like people always do in the movies, though what good that would do I couldn't figure, since if something really wanted to get at us, it would just break the window and come in.

"Upstairs," I whispered.

We tiptoed up the stairs. Once we were in our bedroom, I thought we were safe. Crawling over the floor, I raised my head just enough to peek out the window. My heart almost stopped. Standing in the moonlight was an enormous, manlike creature. It had a scrap of cloth in its hands. It was looking around—looking for us. I saw it lift its head and sniff the wind. To my horror, it started back toward the house.

"It's coming back!" I yelped, more frightened than ever.

"How does it know where we are?" asked Marie.

I knew how. It had Duffy's jacket. It was tracking us down, like some giant bloodhound.

We huddled together in the middle of the room, trying to think of what to do.

A minute later we heard it.

Scratch, scratch.

None of us moved.

Scratch, scratch.

We stopped breathing, then jumped up in alarm at a terrible crashing sound.

The door was down.

We hunched back against the wall as heavy footsteps came clomping up the stairs.

I wondered what our mothers would think when they got back. Would they find our bodies? Or would there be nothing left of us at all?

Thump. Thump. Thump.

It was getting closer.

Thump. Thump. Thump.

It was outside the door.

Knock, knock.

"Don't answer!" hissed Duffy.

Like I said, he doesn't have the brains of a turnip.

It didn't matter. The door wasn't locked. It came swinging open. In the shaft of light I saw a huge figure. The Sentinel of the Woods! It had to be. I thought I was going to die.

The figure stepped into the room. Its head nearly touched the ceiling.

Marie squeezed against my side, tighter than a tick in a dog's ear.

The huge creature sniffed the air. It turned in our direction. Its eyes seemed to glow. Moonlight glittered on its fangs.

Slowly the Sentinel raised its arm. I could see Duffy's jacket dangling from its fingertips.

And then it spoke.

"You forgot your jacket, stupid."

It threw the jacket at Duffy, turned around, and stomped down the stairs.

Which is why, I suppose, no one has had to remind Duffy to remember his jacket, or his glasses, or his math book, for at least a year now.

After all, when you leave stuff lying around, you never can be sure just who might bring it back.

Homeward Bound

AMIE STOOD on the steps of his uncle's house and looked up. The place was tall and bleak. With its windows closed and shuttered, as they were now, it was easy to imagine the building was actually trying to keep him out.

"This isn't home," he thought rebelliously. "It's not home, and it never will be."

A pigeon fluttered onto the lawn nearby. Jamie started, then frowned. His father had raised homing pigeons, and the two of them had spent many happy hours together, tending his flock.

But the sight of the bird now, with the loss of his father still so fresh in his mind, only stirred up memories he wasn't yet ready to deal with.

He looked at the house again and was struck by an odd feeling: while this wasn't home, coming here had somehow taken him one step closer to finding it. That feeling had to do with the horn, of course; of that much he was certain.

Jamie was seven the first time he had seen the horn hanging on the wall of his uncle's study.

"Narwhal," said his uncle, following the boy's gaze. "It's a whale with a horn growing out of the front of its head." He put one hand to his forehead and thrust out a finger to illustrate, as if Jamie were some sort of an idiot. "Sort of a seagoing unicorn," he continued. "Except, of course, that it's real instead of imaginary. I'd rather you didn't touch it. I paid dearly to get it."

Jamie had stepped back behind his father without speaking. He hadn't dared to say what was on his mind. Grown-ups, especially his uncle, didn't like to be told they were wrong.

But his uncle *was* wrong. The horn had not come from a narwhal, not come from the sea at all.

It was the horn of a genuine unicorn.

Jamie couldn't have explained how he knew this was so. But he did, as surely—and mysteriously—as his father's pigeons knew their way home. Thinking of that moment of certainty now, he was reminded of those stormy nights when he and his father had watched lightning crackle through the summer sky. For an instant, everything would be outlined in light. Then, just as quickly, the world would be plunged back into darkness, with nothing remaining but a dazzling memory.

That was how it had been with the horn, five years ago.

And now Jamie was twelve, and his father was dead, and he had been sent to live with this rich, remote man who had always frightened him so much.

Oddly, that fear didn't come from his uncle. Despite his stern manner, the man was always quiet and polite with Jamie. Rather he had learned the fear from his father. The two men had not been together often, for his uncle frequently disappeared on mysterious "business trips" lasting weeks or even months on end. But as Jamie had watched his father grow nervous and unhappy whenever his brother was due to return, he came to sense that the one man had some strange hold over the other.

It frightened him.

Yet as scared as he was, as sad and lonely over the death of his father, one small corner of his soul was burning now with a fierce joy because he was finally going to be close to the horn.

Of course, in a way, he had never been apart

from it. Ever since that first sight, five years ago, the horn had shimmered in his memory. It was the first thing he thought of when he woke up, and the last at night when he went to sleep. It was a gleaming beacon in his dreams, reassuring him no matter how cruel and ugly a day might have been, there was a reason to go on, a reason to be. His one glimpse of the horn had filled him with a sense of beauty and rightness so powerful it had carried him through these five years.

Even now, while his uncle was droning on about the household rules, he saw it again in that space in the back of his head where it seemed to reside. Like a shaft of never-ending light, it tapered through the darkness of his mind, wrist thick at its base, ice-pick sharp at its tip, a spiraled wonder of icy, pearly whiteness. And while Jamie's uncle was telling him the study was off-limits, Jamie was trying to figure out how quickly he could slip in there to see the horn again.

For once again his uncle was wrong. No place that held the horn could be off-limits for him. It was too deeply a part of him.

That was why he had come here so willingly, despite his fear of his uncle. Like the pigeons, he was making his way home.

Jamie listened to the big clock downstairs as it marked off the quarter hours. When the house had been quiet for seventy-five minutes he took the flashlight from under his pillow, climbed out of bed, and slipped on his robe. Walking softly, he made his way down the hall, enjoying the feel of the thick carpet like moss beneath his feet.

He paused at the door of the study. Despite his feelings, he hesitated. What would his uncle say, or do, if he woke and caught him here?

The truth was, it didn't matter. He had no choice. He had to see the horn again.

Turning the knob of the door, he held his breath against the inevitable click. But when it came, it was mercifully soft. He stepped inside and flicked on his flashlight.

His heart lurched as the beam struck the opposite wall and showed an empty place where the horn had once hung. A little cry slipped through his lips before he remembered how important it was to remain silent.

He swung the light around the room, and breathed a sigh of relief. The horn—the alicorn, as his reading had told him it was called—lay across his uncle's desk.

He stepped forward, almost unable to believe that the moment he had dreamed of all these years was finally at hand.

He took another step, and another.

He was beside the desk now, close enough to reach out and touch the horn.

And still he hesitated.

Part of that hesitation came from wonder, for the horn was even more beautiful than he had remembered. Another part of it came from a desire to make this moment last as long as he possibly could. It was something he had been living toward for five years now, and he wanted to savor it. But the biggest part of his hesitation came from fear. He had a sense that once he had touched the horn, his life might never be the same again.

That didn't mean he wouldn't do it.

But he needed to prepare himself. So for a while he simply stood in the darkness, gazing at the horn. Light seemed to play beneath its surface, as if there was something alive inside it— though how that could be after all this time he didn't know.

Finally he reached out to stroke the horn. Just stroke it. He wasn't ready, yet, to truly embrace whatever mystery was waiting for him. Just a hint, just a teasing glimpse, was all he wanted.

His fingertip grazed the horn and he cried out in terror as the room lights blazed on, and his uncle's powerful voice thundered over him, demanding to know what was going on.

Jamie collapsed beside the desk. His uncle scooped him up and carried him back to his room.

A fever set in, and it was three days before Jamie got out of bed again.

He had vague memories of people coming to see him during that time—of a doctor who took his pulse and temperature; of an older woman who hovered beside him, spooning a thin broth between his lips and wiping his forehead with a cool cloth; and most of all of his uncle, who loomed over his bed like a thundercloud, glowering down at him.

His only other memories were of the strange dream that gripped him over and over again, causing him to thrash and cry out in terror. In the dream he was running through a deep forest. Something was behind him, pursuing him. He leaped over mossy logs, splashed through cold streams, crashed through brambles and thickets. But no matter how he tried, he couldn't escape the fierce thing that was after him—a thing that wore his uncle's face.

More than once Jamie sat up in bed, gasping and covered with sweat. Then the old woman, or the doctor, would speak soothing words and try to calm his fears.

Once he woke quietly. He could hear doves cooing outside his window. Looking up, he saw his uncle standing beside the bed, staring down at him angrily.

Why? wondered Jamie. *Why doesn't he want me to touch the horn?*

But he was tired, and the question faded as he slipped back into his dreams.

He was sent away to a school, where he was vaguely miserable but functioned well enough to keep the faculty at a comfortable distance. The other students, not so easily escaped, took some delight in trying to torment the dreamy boy who was so oblivious to their little world of studies and games, their private wars and rages. After a while they gave it up; Jamie didn't react enough to make their tortures worth the effort on any but the most boring of days.

He had other things to think about, memories and mysteries that absorbed him and carried him through the year, aware of the world around him only enough to move from one place to another, to answer questions, to keep people away.

The memories had two sources. The first was the vision that had momentarily dazzled him when he touched the horn, a tantalizing instant of joy so deep and powerful it had shaken him to the roots of his being. Hints of green, of cool, of wind in face and hair whispered at the edges of that vision.

He longed to experience it again.

The other memories echoed from his fever dreams, and were not so pleasant. They spoke only of fear, and some terrible loss he did not understand.

Christmas, when it finally came, was difficult. As the other boys were leaving for home his uncle sent word that urgent business would keep him out of town throughout the holiday. He paid the headmaster handsomely to keep an eye on Jamie and feed him Christmas dinner.

The boy spent a bleak holiday longing for his father. Until now his obsession with the horn had shielded him from the still-raw pain of that loss. But the sounds and smells of the holiday, the tinkling bells, the warm spices, the temporary but real goodwill surrounding him, all stirred the sorrow inside him, and he wept himself to sleep at night.

He dreamed. In his dreams his father would reach out to take his hand. "We're all lost," he would whisper, as he had the day he died. "Lost, and aching to find our name, so that we can finally go home again."

When Jamie woke, his pillow would be soaked with sweat, and tears.

The sorrow faded with the return of the other students, and the resumption of a daily routine. Even so, it was a relief when three months later his uncle sent word that Jamie would be allowed to come back for the spring holiday.

The man made a point of letting Jamie know

he had hidden the horn by taking him into the study soon after the boy's arrival at the house. He watched closely as Jamie's eyes flickered over the walls, searching for the horn, and seemed satisfied at the expression of defeat that twisted his face before he closed in on himself, shutting out the world again.

But Jamie had become cunning. The defeat he showed his uncle was real. What the man didn't see, because the boy buried it as soon as he was aware of it, was that the defeat was temporary. For hiding the horn didn't make any difference. Now that Jamie had touched it, he was bound to it. Wherever it was hidden, he would find it. Its call was too powerful to mistake.

Even so, Jamie thought he might lose his mind before he got his chance. Day after day his uncle stayed in the house, guarding his treasure. Finally, on the morning of the fifth day, an urgent message pulled him away. Even then the anger that burned in his face as he stormed through the great oak doors, an anger Jamie knew was rooted in being called from his vigil, might have frightened someone less determined.

The boy didn't care. He would make his way to the horn while he had the chance.

He knew where it was, of course—had known from the evening of the first day.

It was in his uncle's bedroom.

* * *

The room was locked. Moving cautiously, Jamie slipped downstairs to the servants' quarters and stole the master key, then scurried back to the door. To his surprise he felt no fear.

He decided it was because he had no choice; he was only doing what he had to do.

He twisted the key in the lock and swung the door open.

His uncle's room was large and richly decorated, filled with heavy, carefully carved furniture. Above the dresser hung a huge mirror.

Jamie hesitated for just a moment, then lay on his stomach and peered beneath the bed.

The horn was there, wrapped in a length of blue velvet.

He reached in and drew the package out. Then he stood and placed it gently on the bed. With reverent fingers he unrolled the velvet. Cradled by the rich blue fabric, the horn looked like a comet blazing across a midnight sky.

This time there could be no interruption. Hesitating for no more than a heartbeat, he reached out and clutched the horn with both hands.

He cried out, in agony, and in awe. For a moment he thought he was going to die. The feelings the horn unleashed within him seemed too much for his body to hold. He didn't die, though his heart was racing faster than it had any right to.

"More," he thought, as images of the place he had seen in his dreams rushed through his mind. "I have to know more."

He drew the horn to his chest and laid his cheek against it.

He thought his heart would beat its way out of his body.

And still it wasn't enough.

He knew what he had to do next. But he was afraid.

Fear made no difference. He remembered again what his father had said about people aching to find their true name. He was close to his now. *No one can come this close and not reach out for the answer,* he thought. *The emptiness would kill them on the spot.*

And so he did what he had to do, fearful as it was. Placing the base of the horn against the foot of the massive bed, he set the tip of it against his heart.

Then he leaned forward.

The point of the horn pierced his flesh like a sword made of fire and ice. He cried out, first in pain, then in joy and wonder. Finally the answer was clear to him, and he understood his obsession, and his loneliness.

"No wonder I didn't fit," he thought, as his fingers fused, then split into cloven hooves.

The transformation was painful. But the joy so far surpassed it that he barely noticed the fire he felt as his neck began to stretch, and the horn erupted from his brow. "No wonder, no wonder—no, it's all wonder, wonder, wonder and joy!"

He reared back in triumph, his silken mane streaming behind him, as he trumpeted the joyful discovery that he was, and always had been, and always would be, a unicorn.

And knowing his name, he finally knew how to go home. Hunching the powerful muscles of his hind legs, he launched himself toward the dresser. His horn struck the mirror, and it shattered into a million pieces that crashed and tinkled into two different worlds.

He hardly noticed. He was through, and home at last.

No, said a voice at the back of his head. *You're not home yet.*

He stopped. It was true. He wasn't home yet, though he was much closer. But there was still more to do, and further to go.

How could that be? He knew he was, had always been, a unicorn. Then he trembled, as he realized his father's last words were still true. There was something inside that needed to be discovered, to be named.

He whickered nervously as he realized all he had really done was come back to where most people begin—his own place, his own shape.

He looked around. He was standing at the edge

of a clearing in an old oak wood. Sunlight filtered through the leaves, dappling patches of warmth onto his flanks. He paused for a moment, taking pleasure in feeling his own true shape at last.

Suddenly he shivered, then stood stock-still as the smell of the girl reached his nostrils.

The scent was sweet, and rich, and he could resist it no more than he had resisted the horn. He began trotting in her direction, sunlight bouncing off the horn that jutted out from his forehead.

He found her sitting beneath an apple tree, singing to herself while she brushed her honey-colored hair. Doves rustled and cooed at the edges of the clearing. They reminded him of the pigeons his father had raised.

As he stood and watched her, every fiber of his being cried out that there was danger here. But it was not in the nature of a unicorn to resist such a girl.

Lowering his head, he walked forward.

"So," she said. "You've come at last."

He knelt beside her, and she began to stroke his mane. Her fingers felt cool against his neck, and she sang to him in a voice that seemed to wash away old sorrows. He relaxed into a sweet silence, content for the first time that he could remember.

He wanted the moment to go on forever.

But it ended almost instantly as the girl slipped

a golden bridle over his head, and his uncle suddenly stepped into the clearing.

The man was wearing a wizard's garb, which didn't surprise Jamie. Ten armed soldiers stood behind him.

Jamie sprang to his feet. But he had been bound by the magic of the bridle; he could neither run, nor attack.

Flanks heaving, he stared at his wizard uncle.

"Did you really think you could get away from me?" asked the man.

I have! thought Jamie fiercely, knowing the thought would be understood.

"Don't be absurd!" snarled his uncle. "I'll take your horn, as I did your father's. And then I'll take your shape, and finally your memory. You'll come back with me and be no different than he was—a dreamy, foolish mortal, lost and out of place."

Why? thought Jamie. *Why would anyone want to hold a unicorn?*

His uncle didn't answer.

Jamie locked eyes with him, begging him to explain.

No answer came. But he realized he had found a way to survive. Just as the golden bridle held him helpless, so his gaze could hold his uncle. As long as he could stare into the man's eyes, he could keep him from moving.

He knew, too, that as soon as he flinched, the battle would be over.

Jamie had no idea how long the struggle actually lasted. They seemed to be in a place apart, far away from the clearing, away from the girl and the soldiers.

He began to grow fearful. Sooner or later he would falter and his uncle would regain control. It wasn't enough to hold him. He had to conquer him.

But how? *How?*

He couldn't win unless he knew why he was fighting. He had to discover why his uncle wanted to capture and hold him.

But the only way to do that was to look deeper inside the man. The idea frightened him; he didn't know what he would find there. Even worse, it would work two ways. He couldn't look deeper into his uncle, without letting his uncle look more deeply into him.

He hesitated. But there was no other way. Accepting the risk, he opened himself to his uncle.

At the same time he plunged into the man's soul.

His uncle cried out, then dropped to his knees and buried his face in his hands, trembling with the humiliation of being seen.

Jamie trembled too, for the emptiness he

found inside this man could swallow suns and devour planets. This was the hunger that had driven him to capture unicorns, in the hope that their glory could fill his darkness.

Then, at last, Jamie knew what he must do. Stepping forward, he pressed the tip of his horn against his uncle's heart.

He had been aware of his horn's healing power, of course. But this was the first time he had tried to use it. He wasn't expecting the shock of pain that jolted through him, or the wave of despair that followed as he took in the emptiness, and the fear and the hunger that had driven his uncle for so long.

He wanted to pull away, to run in terror.

But if he did, it would only start all over again. Only a healing would put an end to the pursuit. And this was the only way to heal this man, this wizard, who, he now understood, had never really been his uncle, but only his captor. He had to be seen, in all his sorrow and his ugliness; seen, and accepted, and loved. Only then could he be free of the emptiness that made him want to possess a unicorn.

Jamie trembled as the waves of emptiness and sorrow continued to wash through him. But at last he was nearly done. Still swaying from the effort, he whispered to the man: "Go back. Go back and find your name. And then—go *home.*"

That was when the sword fell, slicing through his neck.

It didn't matter, really, though he felt sorry for his "uncle," who began to weep, and sorrier still for the soldier who had done the deed. He knew it would be a decade or so before the man could sleep without mind-twisting nightmares of the day he had killed a unicorn.

But for Jamie himself, the change made no difference. Because he still was what he had always been, what he always would be, what a unicorn had simply been an appropriate shape to hold. He was a being of power and light.

He shook with delight as he realized that he had named himself at last.

He turned to the wizard, and was amazed. No longer hampered by mere eyes, he could see that the same thing was true for his enemy—as it was for the girl, as it was for the soldiers.

They were *all* beings of power and light.

The terrible thing was, they didn't know it.

Suddenly he understood. This was the secret, the unnamed thing his father had been trying to remember: that we are all beings of power and light. And all the pain, all the sorrow—it all came from not knowing this simple truth.

Why? wondered Jamie. *Why don't any of us know how beautiful we really are?*

And then even that question became unimportant, because his father had come to take him home, and suddenly he wasn't just a unicorn, but was all unicorns, was part of every wise and daring being that had worn that shape and that name, every unicorn that had ever lived, or ever would live. And he felt himself stretch to fill the sky, as the stars came tumbling into his body, stars at his knees and at his hooves, at his shoulder and his tail, and most of all a shimmer of stars that lined the length of his horn, a horn that stretched across the sky, pointing out, for anyone who cared to look, the way to go home.

With His Head
Tucked Underneath
His Arm

FIFTEEN KINGS ruled the continent of Losfar, and each one hated the others. Old, fat, and foolish, they thought nothing of sending the children of their subjects off on war after war after war, so that the best and the bravest were gone to dust before they ever really lived.

The young men left behind fell into two groups: those who escaped the wars for reasons of the body—the weak, the crippled, the maimed—and those who avoided the wars for reasons of the mind; those too frightened, too smart, or simply too loving to be caught in the trap the kings laid for them.

This last category was smallest of all, and a dangerous one to be in. Questioning the wars outright was against the law, and standing up to declare they were wrong was a quick route to the dungeons that lay beneath the palace. So it was only through deceit that those who opposed the wars could escape going off to kill people they had never met, and had nothing against.

One such was a cobbler's son named Brion, who had avoided the wars by walking on a crutch and pretending that he was crippled. Yet he chafed under the role he played, for he was not the sort to live a lie.

"Why do I have to pretend?" he would ask his friend Mikel, an older man who was one of the few who knew his secret. "Why must I lie, when I am right, and they are wrong?"

But Mikel had no answer. And since much as Brion hated the lie, he hated even more the idea of killing some stranger for the sake of a war he did not believe in, he continued to pretend.

One afternoon when Brion was limping through the marketplace on his crutch, he saw an officer of the king's army beating a woman because she had fallen in his path. The sight angered him so much that without thinking he stepped in to help the woman. "Leave her alone!" he cried, grabbing the officer's arm.

The man pushed Brion away and raised his hand to strike the woman again.

"Help!" she wailed. "He's killing me!"

Brion hesitated for but a moment. Though he knew it would reveal his lie, he sprang to his feet and felled the man with a single blow.

In an instant he was surrounded by soldiers.

Within an hour he found himself chained to a dungeon wall, with no one for company save the occasional passing rat, and no music save the trickle of the water that dripped endlessly down the cold stones.

As the days went by Brion began to wonder if he had been forgotten and would simply be left in his cell to rot. But late one afternoon he heard the clink of keys in the lock. Two uniformed men came into his cell, unlocked his chains, and dragged him to his feet. Gripping his arms in their mailed gloves, they hustled him to the throne room, to face the king.

"Is it true that you refuse to fight for me?" asked the king angrily.

At the moment, Brion's main fight was with the lump of fear lodged in his throat. But he stood as straight as he was able and said, "It is true. I cannot kill a man I have never met for the sake of a war I do not believe in."

The king's jowly face grew scarlet with rage.

"Let the court see the treason of this speech. Let it be recorded, so that all will understand why this rebellious youth is being put to death."

Three days later Brion was marched to the public square. His weeping mother stood at the front of the crowd, shaking with sorrow as the guards escorted her son up the steps to die. Pushed to his knees, Brion laid his head on the block. He heard his father's voice cry out. But the words were lost to him, because the executioner's ax had fallen.

The crowd roared as Brion's severed head tumbled into the waiting basket.

Body and head were buried in a shallow grave far outside the city, in a corner of the boneyard reserved for traitors.

Brion was about as mad as a dead man can be, which may explain why three nights later he climbed out of the ground. Reaching back, he plucked his head from the grave, gave it a shake to rid it of loose dirt, then tucked it under his arm and started for the city.

It was the quietest part of the night when he reached the palace. Most of the guards were nodding at their posts, but even the few who were still alert did not see him enter.

The dead have their ways.

Slowly Brion climbed the stairs to the king's bedchamber. When he entered the room he stood in silence. But his presence alone was enough to trouble the king, and after a moment the fat old man sat up suddenly, crying, "Who dares to disturb my sleep?"

"I dare," said Brion, "because I know you for what you really are: a murderer and a thief, not fit to be king. You have been stealing your subjects' lives, and I have come to set things right."

Then he crossed the room and stood in a shaft of moonlight that flowed through the window next to the king's bed. When the king saw the body of the young man he had ordered killed just three days earlier standing next to him, saw the severed head with its still-raw wound, he began to scream.

"Silence!" ordered Brion, raising his head to hold it before the king's face. "Silence, if you wish to see the morning!"

Trembling beneath his blankets, the king pleaded with Brion to spare his life. "I will do anything you ask," he whimpered. "Anything at all."

The head smiled. Then Brion told the king what he wanted him to do.

The next day the king's advisors were astonished to hear the king announce that the war was over, and that he was calling the armies back from the field.

"Why, your majesty?" they asked. They were deeply disturbed, for they loved their game of war and were sad to see it end.

But the king would say nothing of his reasons. Now life in the kingdom began to change slowly for the better. The youths who returned from the war began to take a useful part in the life of their homeland. With strong young hands to till the fields, the farms grew more productive. Some of those who returned from the wars were artists and poets; some were builders and thinkers. New ideas came forward, new designs, new ways of doing things. As time went on the kingdom grew stronger, happier, and more prosperous than any of those surrounding it.

And in all this time Brion never left the king to himself. Though the guard was doubled, and doubled again, somehow they always slept when Brion walked the halls—as he did every night when he came to visit the king's bedchamber. And there, with his head tucked underneath his arm, he would instruct the king on what to do next.

When morning came, Brion would be gone. But the smell of death lingered in the room. The servants began to whisper that the king was ailing, and would not live much longer. But live he did, and for the next three years he continued to do as Brion told him.

In that time the kingdom grew so prosperous

that the other kings on Losfar grew jealous. They began to plot together and soon decided to attack the rebellious kingdom that had left the wars.

"After all," said King Fulgram, "the only reason they have so much is that they have not been spending it to defend themselves, as have we. Therefore, a share of it should be ours."

"A *large* share," said King Nichard with a smile.

When Brion heard that the armies of Losfar were marching on his homeland, he did not know what to do. He certainly did not want a war. But neither did he want to let the outsiders tear down all that had been built. And he knew he could not let them murder his people.

"Send a message of peace to the enemy camp," he told the king a few nights before the enemy was expected to arrive.

The king sneered, but, as always, did as he was told.

The messenger was murdered, his body sent back as a warning of what was to come.

Panic swept the kingdom.

That night, when Brion stood by the king's bedside, the old man began to gloat over the coming war. "See what you have brought us to," he taunted. "We are no better off, and in fact far worse, than when you started. Before, we fought on *their* soil, and it was *their* homes that were destroyed. In two days' time the enemy will be upon us, and this time it is *our* city that will burn."

Brion said nothing, for he did not know what to do.

Later, when he was walking back to his grave, Brion met another traveler on the road. Brion recognized him as the murdered messenger by the stray bits of moonlight that flowed through the holes in his chest (for the king had described the man's wounds with savage delight).

The messenger turned from his path to walk with Brion. For a time the two men traveled in silence.

Brion felt a great sorrow, for he blamed himself for the messenger's death. Finally he began to speak, and told the man everything that had happened since his own beheading.

"Don't feel bad," replied the messenger. "After all, your heart was in the right place—which is more than I can say for your head," he added, gesturing to the grisly object Brion carried beneath his arm. It was sadly battered now, for dead flesh does not heal, and in three years it had suffered many small wounds and bruises.

Brion's head began to laugh, and before long the two dead men were staggering along the road, leaning on each other as they told bad jokes about death and dying.

After a time they paused. Standing together, they stared into the deep and starry sky.

"I am so tired," said Brion at last. "How I wish that I could be done with this. How I wish that I could rest."

"You cannot," said the messenger. "You must finish what you have started."

Brion sighed, for he knew that his new friend was right. "And what of you?" he asked. "Why do you walk this night?"

"I was too angry to rest," said the messenger. "I wish that those fools could know how sweet life is. But perhaps only the dead can know that."

"More's the pity," said Brion. And with that he left the messenger and returned to his grave.

But the messenger's words stayed with him, and the next night when he rose, he knew what to do. Finding the grave of the messenger, he called him forth, saying, "I have one last messenge for you to deliver."

Then he told him his plan. Smiling, the messenger agreed to help. And so the two men went from grave to grave, calling the dead with these words:

"Awake, arise! Your children are in danger, your parents may perish, your childhood homes will burn. All that you loved in life is at peril. Awake, arise, and walk with us."

Not every soul gave back an answer. Some were too long dead, or too tired, or too far away in the next world. Some had never cared about these things in life. But for many, Brion's call was all that was needed to stir them from their place of rest. The earth began to open, and up from their graves rose the young and the old, the long dead and the newly buried. And each that rose took up the message and went to gather others, so that two became four, and four became eight, and eight became a multitude, shaking the earth from their dead and rotted limbs for the sake of all that they had loved in life.

When the army of the dead had gathered at the gate of the graveyard, Brion stood before them and took his head from beneath his arm. Holding it high, he told them all that had happened.

He told them what he wanted of them.

Then he turned and headed for the camp of the enemy.

Behind him marched the army of the dead. Some moaned as they traveled, remembering the sweetness and the sorrow of the living world. Some were no more than skeletons, their bones stripped clean by their years in the earth. Others, more recently dead, left bits and pieces of themselves along the way.

Soon they reached the camp of the enemy, which was all too close to the city. Following Brion's lead, they entered the camp. It was easy enough to pass the sentries. The dead *do* have their ways. Then, by ones and twos, they entered the tents of the living, where they began to sing to them of death's embrace.

"Look on me, look on me," they whispered in the ears of the sleeping men. "As I am, soon you shall be."

When the soldiers roused from their dreams of killing and dying to find themselves looking into the faces of those already dead, fear crept into their hearts.

But the dead meant them no harm. They had come only to speak to them, slowly and softly, of what it is to be dead; how it feels to be buried in the earth; what it is like to have worms burrow through your body.

"This will come to you soon enough," they whispered, extending their cold hands to stroke the faces of the living.

Some of the dead women held out their arms. When the men cried out and cowered from their touch, they whispered, "If you fear my embrace, then fear the grave as well. Go home, go home, and there do good. Choose life, choose life, and leave this place in peace."

One by one, the terrified men slipped from their tents and fled across the hills to their homes, until the invading army had vanished like a ghost in the night.

Then the army of the dead returned to the

cemetery. They laughed as they went, and were well pleased, and chuckled at their victory. For though they had spoken nothing but the truth, they had not told all that there was to tell. The departing men would learn that in good time; there was no need for them to know *all* the secrets of the world beyond too soon.

As dawn drew near, Brion stood at the edge of his grave and stared into it with longing. At last the time had come to discover what came next, the secrets and surprises he had denied himself for three long years.

Tenderly he placed his head in the grave. Then crawling in beside it, he laid himself down and died.

Clean as a Whistle

JAMIE CARHART was, quite possibly, the messiest kid in Minnesota. The messiest kid in her town, no doubt. The county? She pretty well had that sewed up, too. And her mother was convinced that, were there a statewide competition, Jamie would easily be in the top ten, and might, indeed, take first place.

Not that Mrs. Carhart was amused by this fact.

"This room is a sty!" she would say at least once a day, standing in the doorway of Jamie's room and sighing. Then she would poke her foot at the mess that threatened to creep out into the rest of the house, sigh again as if the whole thing was far too much for her to cope with, and wander off.

So it was a shock for Jamie to come home from school on the afternoon of April 17 and find her room totally, perfectly, absolutely neat, clean, and tidy.

"Aaaaaah!" she cried, standing in her doorway. "Aaaaaah! What happened? Who did this?"

Jamie didn't really expect an answer. Her parents both worked and wouldn't be home for another two hours.

For a horrible moment she wondered if her grandmother had come to visit. Gramma Hattie was perfectly capable of sneaking into a kid's room and cleaning it while that kid wasn't looking. Heaven alone knew where *she* might have put things. Even Jamie's mother found Gramma Hattie hard to cope with.

But Gramma Hattie lived in Utah (which in Jamie's opinion was a good place for her), and now that Jamie thought of it, she was off on a trip to Europe. Besides, if she had done this, she would have pounced by now, crowing at her victory over disorder.

So it wasn't her.

Jamie hesitated, wondering if she dared go in.

"Anyone here?" she asked timidly.

No answer.

"Anyone?"

Silence, though she did notice that the cat was on her bed. This did not please her. Actually, she always longed to have the cat in her room. But Mr. Bumpo normally refused to come through her door. Jamie's mother claimed this was because the cat was too neat and couldn't stand the mess. Jamie denied this, usually quite angrily. So she wasn't amused to find Mr. Bumpo here now that the room was so clean; his gently purring presence seemed to confirm her mother's horrible theory.

Jamie looked around nervously as she entered the room. After a moment she dropped her books on her bed. She waited, half expecting someone to come dashing in and pick them up.

"What is going on here?" she asked the cat, scratching its orange-and-black head.

Mr. Bumpo closed his eyes and purred louder.

When Mrs. Carhart arrived home and came up to say hello to Jamie, she grabbed the edges of the doorway and staggered as if she had been hit between the eyes with a two-by-four.

"What," she asked in astonishment, "got into you?"

"What are you talking about?" asked Jamie sourly. She was sitting at her desk, working on a small clay project. She had generated a minor mess with the work, and managed to create a tad of clutter here and there. But overall the room was still so clean as to be unrecognizable.

"I mean this room," said her mother. She squeezed her eyes shut then opened them again, as if to make sure that she wasn't hallucinating. "It's so . . . so . . . *tidy!*"

Jamie looked at her suspiciously. "Didn't you hire someone to come in here and clean it?" she asked. She was still fairly angry about the invasion of her privacy (and not about to admit that she was delighted to find her clay-working tools, which had been missing for some six months now).

Her mother snorted. "The day we can afford a housekeeper, he or she takes on some of *my* work first."

"Then who did this to me?" asked Jamie.

Her mother looked at her oddly. "You are the strangest child," she said at last. "But thanks anyway."

Before Jamie could reply, Mrs. Carhart turned and left. Jamie growled and stabbed a long metal tool through the little clay man she had been making. She knew what her mother was thinking. She was thinking that she, Jamie, had cleaned up the room but was too embarrassed to admit it. She was also thinking that if she pushed the issue Jamie would never do it again. Which meant that when Jamie claimed she had nothing to do with this . . . this *catastrophe,* her mother would simply think that she was playing an odd game, and the more she tried to convince her otherwise, the more Mrs. Carhart would be convinced that she was right in her assumption. Jamie groaned. It was hopeless.

Of course, the other possibility was that her mother was lying and really had hired someone to clean the room. Jamie considered the idea. "Unlikely," she said out loud.

But what other explanation was there? Some demented prowler who broke into people's houses to clean rooms when no one was at home? Jamie glanced around nervously, then shook her head.

Dinner that night was interesting. Mrs. Carhart had clearly warned Mr. Carhart that he was not to make a big deal over the clean room for fear that Jamie would never do it again.

By the time the meal was over, Jamie wanted to scream.

By the time the night was over, she *did* scream. "I just want you to know that I am *not* responsible for this!" she bellowed, standing at the top of the stairs. "I had nothing to do with it!"

She heard her father chuckle.

Furious, she returned to her room, slamming

the door behind her. When she undressed for bed she tore off her clothes and scattered them about the floor. Once she was in her nightgown she went to the door, opened it a crack, and yelled "Good night!"

Then she slammed it shut and climbed between the sheets.

When Jamie got home the next afternoon, yesterday's clothes (which she had studiously avoided touching that morning) had disappeared from her floor. Her clay-working tools were lined up in an orderly fashion on her desk. The bits of clay that she had left around had been gathered together and rolled into a ball.

The cat was curled up in the middle of her bed, sleeping peacefully.

"Did you do this?" she asked, looking at him suspiciously. She was perfectly aware of what a stupid question it was. On the other hand, when things got this weird, stupid questions began to make sense.

Mr. Bumpo blinked at her, but said nothing. She reached out to stroke him and realized that his fur, which normally had a number of tangles and knots, was perfectly groomed.

"This is creepy," she said. "And I don't like it." She tossed her backpack on the bed and began to search the room for some clue or sign as to who might have done this. Under her bed she found only that the rapidly breeding colony of dust bunnies had become extinct. She checked her closet next, where she saw something she had not laid eyes on in over three years: the floor. When she looked in her dresser she found that every item of clothing had been neatly folded. This was even worse than it had been the day before!

What she did not find was any sign of who had done this terrible thing to her.

She sat on the edge of her bed for a long time, stroking Mr. Bumpo and listening to him purr. Finally she decided to go back to her clay working. Remembering a sketch for a new project she had made during math class, she overturned her pack and emptied it on the bed. Out tumbled a mixture of books, crumpled papers, pens and pencils in various stages of usefulness, candy wrappers, rubber bands, sparkly rocks she had picked up on the way to and from school, three crayons stuck together with a piece of used chewing gum, and a moldy sandwich.

Jamie dug her way through the mound of stuff until she found the sketch. She carried it to her desk and smoothed it out, then picked up the ball of clay and began to work. After about half an hour she decided to go get a snack.

When she got up from her desk and turned around she let out a yelp of astonishment.

Her bed was perfectly clean! The mess she had dumped onto it had been organized and tidied into meek submission. The crumpled papers had vanished, the pencils were lined up in a tidy row, the crayons unstuck, the gum that held them together mysteriously gone. Even the backpack's straps had been neatly folded beneath it.

"What is going on here?" she cried.

The only answer was a yawn from Mr. Bumpo.

Goose bumps prickling over her arms, Jamie wondered if she should run for her life. But nothing about what was happening was threatening. It was just . . . *weird.*

She stared at her bed for a while, then made a decision. Stomping over to it, she snatched up the neat piles and tossed them into the air. Mr. Bumpo yowled in alarm, bolted from the bed, and ran out of the room. Jamie stirred the mess around a bit more, rumpled the bedcovers for good measure, then went back to her desk and picked up her tools. She pretended to work. What she was really doing was trying to look over her shoulder while bending her neck as little as possible.

For several minutes nothing happened except that her neck got sore. In a way, she was glad nothing happened; part of her had been afraid of what she might see. Eventually the pain in her neck got to be too much, and she was forced to straighten her head. When she turned back she saw a brown blur out of the corner of her eye.

"Gotcha!" she cried, leaping to her feet.

But whatever it was had disappeared.

Jamie stood still for a moment, wondering what had happened. *Under the bed!* she thought suddenly.

Dropping to her knees, she crept to the bed and lifted the edge of the spread. All she saw was clean floor, and a ripple of movement at the other side of the spread. Whatever had been there had escaped.

"That little stinker is fast," Jamie muttered, getting to her feet. She stared at the bed, which was still a mess, and made a decision. Leaving the room, she headed for the kitchen.

When Jamie returned to her room the bed had been remade and the things from her pack were in perfect order. This did not surprise her.

She went to the far side of the bed, the side from which whatever-it-was had disappeared. She opened the bottle of molasses she had taken from the kitchen, then poured a thick line of the sticky goo the length of the bed, about a foot from the edge. Replacing the lid, she once again messed up everything on top of the bed. Then she returned to her desk.

It wasn't long before she heard a tiny voice cry, "What have you done, what have you done?"

Turning, she saw a manlike creature about a foot-and-a-half tall. He was jumping up and down beside her bed. Covered with brown fur, he looked like a tiny, potbellied version of Bigfoot. The main differences were a long tail and a generally more human face.

"Wretched girl!" cried the creature, shaking a hazelnut-sized fist at her. "What's the matter wi' you?"

"What's the matter with *you?*" she replied. "Sneaking into a person's room and cleaning it up when you're not invited is perverted."

"I was too invited," snapped the creature. Sitting down, he flicked his tail out of the way and began licking molasses from the bottom of his right foot.

"What a liar you are!" said Jamie.

"What a Messy Carruthers you are!" replied the creature. "And you don't know everything, miss. I was sent here by one of your blood. That counts as invitation if she is close enough— which she is."

Jamie scowled, then her eyes opened wide. "My grandmother!" she exclaimed. *"She* sent you, didn't she?"

"That she did, and I can see why, too. Really, this place is quite pathetic. I don't understand why you wouldn't welcome having someone clean it up. I should think you'd be grateful."

"This is my room, and I liked it the way it was," said Jamie.

This was not entirely true. Jamie did sometimes wish that the place was clean. But she felt that she couldn't admit that without losing the argument altogether. Besides, she mostly did like it her way; and she most certainly did *not* like having someone clean it without her permission. She felt as if she had been robbed or something. "What are you, anyway?" she asked, by way of changing the topic.

The creature rolled his eyes, as if he couldn't believe her stupidity. "I'm a brownie," he said. "As any fool can plainly see."

"Brownies don't exist."

"Rude!" cried the creature. "Rude, rude, rude! Your grandmother warned me about that. 'She's a rude girl,' she said. And she was right."

"I think it was rude of my grandmother to talk about me like that in front of a complete stranger," replied Jamie.

"I'm not a complete stranger. I've been the MacDougal family brownie for nearly three hundred years."

"That shows what you know!" said Jamie. "I'm not a MacDougal, I'm a Carhart."

"Aye, and what was your mother's name before she was married?"

"Chase," said Jamie smugly.

"And her mother's name?"

Jamie's sense of certainty began to fade. "I don't have the slightest idea," she said irritably.

"Rude, and irreverent as well! No sense of family, have you girl? Well, I'll tell you what you should have known all along. Your grandmother's maiden name was MacDougal—Harriet Hortense MacDougal, to be precise."

"What has that got to do with me?" asked Jamie.

"Everything," said the brownie. Having finished licking the molasses from his feet, he scooted over to her desk. Moving so fast she barely had time to flinch, he climbed the desk leg and positioned himself in front of her, which made them face-to-face (though his face was barely the size of her fist). "The last of your family in the old country died last year, leaving me without a family to tend to. Your grandmother, bless her heart, came to close up the house. There she found me, moaning and mournful. 'Why brownie,' she says (she being smart enough to know what I am, unlike some I could mention), 'Why brownie, whatever is the matter with you?'

"'My family is all gone,' I told her. 'And now I've naught to care for, so I shall soon fade away.'

"Well, right off your grandmother says, 'Oh, the family is not all gone. I've a daughter in the

States, and *she* has a daughter who could more than use your services.'"

"Thanks, Gramma," muttered Jamie.

"I wasn't much interested in coming to this barbarian wilderness," said the brownie, ignoring the interruption. "But things being what they were, I didn't have much choice. So here I am, much to your good fortune."

Jamie wondered for a moment why Gramma Hattie had sent the brownie to her instead of to her mother. It didn't take her long to figure out the answer. Jamie's mother would have been as happy to have someone clean her house as Jamie was annoyed by having her room invaded. Gramma Hattie would never have wanted to do anything that pleasant.

"What will it take to get you to leave me alone?" she asked.

The brownie began to laugh. "What a silly girl you are!" he cried. "You won't ever be alone again!"

Great, thought Jamie, rolling her eyes. *My grandmother has sent me an eighteen-inch-high stalker.* Aloud, she asked, "Are you saying I don't have any choice in this?"

"It's a family matter," replied the brownie. "No one gets to choose when it comes to things like that."

"But I don't want you here!"

The brownie's lower lip began to quiver and his homely little face puckered into what Jamie's mother called "a booper."

"You really don't want me?" he asked, sniffing just a bit.

Jamie felt her annoyance begin to melt, until she realized what the brownie was trying to do to her. (It wasn't hard to figure it out, since she tried the same thing on her parents often enough.) "Oh, stop it," she snapped.

Instantly the brownie's expression changed. Crossing his arms, he sat down on her desk and said, "I'm staying, and that's final."

"You're going, and I mean it," replied Jamie. But she realized even as she said it that she had no way to make the threat stick. The smug look on the brownie's face told her that he was well aware of this.

Now what was she going to do? Totally frustrated, she said, "I'm going to tell my mother about you." She hated talking like that; it made her feel like a little kid. But she couldn't think of anything else.

It didn't make any difference. "She won't believe you," said the brownie, looking even smugger.

"Wouldn't you like to go to work for her?" pleaded Jamie. "She'd be more than happy to have you."

The brownie looked wistful. "I would be delighted," he replied. "But the oldest female in the family has assigned me to you. I have no choice in the matter."

For a day or two Jamie thought she might be able to live with the situation—though with the brownie taking up residence in her closet she made it a point to do her dressing and undressing in the bathroom.

The worst thing was the way her mother smiled whenever she passed the room. Jamie ground her teeth, but said nothing.

By the third day she was getting used to having the room neat and clean. And though she hated to admit it, it was easier to get things done when she didn't have to spend half an hour looking for whatever she needed to start. But just when she was beginning to think that things might work out, the brownie did something unforgivable.

He began to nag.

"Can't you do anything for yourself?" he asked petulantly when she tossed her books on the bed one afternoon after she arrived home from school. "Am I expected to take care of *everything* around here?"

Jamie looked at him in astonishment. "I didn't ask you to come here!" she exploded. "And I certainly didn't ask you to be messing around with my stuff all the time!"

"I am not messing," said the brownie primly. "I am *un*messing."

"I don't care!" she screamed. "I want you to go away. I don't like having you here all the time. I don't like knowing you're in my closet. I don't like having my room look the way you and my grandmother think it should look instead of the way I think it should look."

"Messy Carruthers," muttered the brownie.

"Nosey Parker!" snapped Jamie, accidentally using one of her grandmother's favorite phrases.

She stomped to her desk. The brownie disappeared into the closet. A heavy silence descended on the room, broken only when Jamie crumpled a sketch she didn't like and tossed it on the floor.

"You pick that up right now!" called the brownie.

Not only did she not pick up the paper, she crumpled another and threw it on the floor just to spite the creature.

That was the beginning of what Jamie later thought of as "The Great Slob War."

Immediately the brownie came dashing from the closet, snatched up the offending papers, and tossed them into the wastebasket. Muttering angrily, he stomped back to the closet (not very effective for someone only a foot and a half tall) and slammed the door behind him.

Jamie immediately wadded up another paper and threw it on the floor. The brownie dashed out to pick it up. Seized by inspiration, Jamie overturned her wastebasket and shook it out. As the brownie began scurrying around to pick up the papers, she plunked the wastebasket down and sat on it. "Now where will you put the papers?" she asked triumphantly.

Her sense of victory dissolved when the brownie gathered the trash in a pile and began to race around it. With a sudden snap, the pile vanished into nothingness. Wiping his hands, the brownie gave her the smuggest look yet. Then he returned to the closet, slamming the door behind him.

"How did you do that?" cried Jamie. He didn't answer. She threw the wastebasket at the door and began to plan her next attack.

She smeared clay on the wall.

She emptied the contents of her dresser onto her floor, tossing out socks, underwear, blouses, and jeans with wild abandon. She tracked all over them with muddy boots and crushed cracker crumbs on top. The brownie simply waited until she left for school. By the time she got home everything had been cleaned, folded, and replaced, neater than before.

Furious, she opened her pencil sharpener and sprinkled its contents all over her bed, topped them off with pancake syrup, a tangled mass of string, and the collection of paper-punch holes she had been saving all year.

The brownie, equally furious, managed to lick and pluck every one of the shavings from the thick weave of the spread with his tiny fingers. The entire time that he was doing this he muttered and cursed, telling Jamie in no uncertain terms what he thought of her, what a disgrace she was to her family, and to what a bad end she was likely to come.

Jamie tipped back her chair on two legs, lounging unrepentantly. "You missed one," she said when the brownie had finished and was heading back to the closet. He raced back to the bed, but after an intense examination discovered that she had been lying.

"What a wicked girl!" he cried. "Trying to fool a poor brownie that way."

"You're not a poor brownie!" she screamed. "You're a menace!" Suddenly days of frustration began to bubble within her. "I can't stand it!" she cried. "I can't take any more of this. I want you to leave me alone!"

"I can't leave you alone!" shouted the brownie, jumping up and down and waving his tiny fists in the air. "We are bound to each other by ancient ties, by words and deeds, by promises written in blood spilled on your family's land."

"Get out!" cried Jamie. In a frenzy she snatched up an old pillow that had come from her grandmother's house and began smacking it against her bed. The pillow burst open, exploding into a cloud of feathers. "Get out, get out, get out!"

Shrieking with rage, the brownie began trying to pick up the feathers. But the faster he moved the more he sent them drifting away from him. When Jamie saw what was happening she began waving her arms to keep the feathers afloat. The brownie leaped and turned, trying to pluck them from the air. He moved faster and faster, wild, frenzied. Finally he began racing in a circle. He went faster still, until he was little more than a blur to Jamie's eyes. Then, with a sudden *snap!* he vanished, just as the papers had the day before.

Jamie blinked, then began to laugh. She had done it. She had gotten rid of him!

And that should have been that.

But a strange thing happened. As the days went on she began to miss the little creature. Infuriating as he had been, he had also been rather cute. Moreover, the condition of her room began to irritate her.

A week after the brownie vanished she was rooting around in the disarray on her floor, trying to find her clay-working tools, which had been missing for three days. Forty-five minutes of searching had so far failed to turn them up.

"Sometimes I actually wish that brownie had stayed around," she muttered.

From the closet a tiny voice said, "A-hoo."

Jamie stood up. "Is that you, brownie?"

"A-hoo," repeated the voice; it sounded pathetically weak.

Feeling slightly nervous—ever since this started she had not been entirely comfortable with her closet—Jamie went to the door and asked, "Are you in there?"

"A-hoo," said the voice a third time. It seemed to come from the upper shelf.

"Brownie, is that you?"

No answer at all this time.

She ran to her desk. Kicking aside the intervening clutter, she dragged the chair back to the closet. By standing on it, she could reach the upper shelf.

"Brownie?" she called. "Are you there?"

"A-hoo."

The voice was coming from a shoe box. She pulled it from the shelf and looked in. The brownie lay inside. He looked wan and thin, and after a moment she realized to her horror that she could see right through him.

"I thought you had left," she said, her voice thick with guilt.

"I had no place to go." His voice seemed to come from a far-off place. "I am bound to you, and to this house. All I could do was wait to fade away."

An icy fear clenched her heart. "Are you going to die?"

"A-hoo," said the brownie. Then he closed his eyes and turned his head away.

She scrambled from the chair and placed the shoe box on her bed. *I've killed him!* she thought in horror. Reaching into the box, she lifted his tiny form. It was no heavier than the feathers he had been chasing when he had disappeared. She could see her fingers right through his body.

"Don't die," she pleaded. "Don't. Stay with me, brownie. We can work something out."

The brownie's eyelids fluttered.

"I mean it!" said Jamie. "I was actually starting to miss you."

"A-hoo," said the brownie. Opening his eyes, he gazed at her uncomprehendingly. "Oh, it's you," he said at last. Then he lifted his head and looked at her room. He moaned tragically at the disarray and closed his eyes again.

"I'll clean it up," she said hastily. "Just don't die. Promise?"

The brownie coughed and seemed to flicker, as if he was going to vanish altogether. "A-hoo," he said again.

"Watch!" said Jamie. Placing his tiny form

gently on the bed, she began a whirlwind cleaning campaign, moving almost as fast as the brownie himself when he was in a cleaning frenzy. Along the way she found her clay-working tools, the pendant her nice grandmother had sent her, two dollars and forty-seven cents in change, and the missing homework that had cost her an F the day before. She kept glancing at the brownie while she worked and was encouraged to see that he seemed to be getting a little more solid. When she was entirely done she turned around and said, "There! See?"

To her enormous annoyance, the brownie had turned the shoe box over and was sitting on the end of it, looking as solid as a brick and smiling broadly. "Well done!" he said.

"I thought you were dying!" she said angrily.

"I wasn't dying, I was fading. And if you wanted me to live, why are you so angry that I'm alive?"

"Because you were faking!" she snarled.

"I never!" cried the brownie, sounding genuinely offended. "Another few minutes and I would have been gone for good, faded away like a summer breeze, like the last coals in the fire, like dew in the morning sun, like—"

"All right, all right," said Jamie. "I get the picture." She paused. Though she still wasn't sure she believed him, she asked, "What happens when you fade?"

The brownie shivered, and the look of terror on his face was so convincing that she began to suspect that he was telling the truth. "I'm just *gone*," he said.

Jamie shivered too. "Do you really have nowhere else to go?" she asked.

The brownie shook his head. "'Tis you to whom I'm bound, and you with whom I must stay until the day I fade away—or the day you become the oldest female in the family and assign me to someone else of your line."

Jamie sighed. She looked at the pendant, the tools, the change lying on her desk. "If I let you stay will you behave?"

The brownie wrapped his tail around his knees. "I am what I am," he said.

"So am I," she replied.

The brownie looked startled, as if this had not occurred to him before. "Can you help a little?" he asked plaintively.

"If I do, will you stop nagging me?"

The brownie considered this for a moment. "Will you let me keep the closet as neat as I want?"

"Can I have my desk as messy as I want?" replied Jamie.

The brownie glanced at the desk, shivered, then nodded.

"It's a deal," said Jamie.

And so it was. They did not, it should be

noted, exactly live happily ever after. The truth is, they annoyed each other a great deal over the years. However, they also learned to laugh together, and had enormous good times when they weren't fighting.

That's the way it goes with family things.

The Language of Blood

GREETINGS, YOUNG ONE. I understand it is your turn, and they have sent you to me to learn how it is. They want me to tell you how I, Banang, came to be the one who speaks the language of blood. They want me to tell you what it cost me, and why I did it.

All right, that's fair. If you are to take my place, these are things you need to know. Take a cushion—one only!—and sit here.

I will tell you the story.

*   *   *

I was born outside the Glorious City. However, my parents moved within its walls before I was a year old. My mother was the ambitious one, always looking for something better. My father was a scribe. From what the elders later told me, the village missed him greatly when he came here. There, he had been the only scribe; here, he was but one among many. But as I said, my mother was ambitious.

I grew up running through the streets of the Glorious City. The neighbors all knew me, and liked me. "There goes Banang," they would say, laughing as I went racing by. "Always running! I'll wager he is the fastest boy in the city." Perhaps I was. But as I found—as you will find, my young friend—you cannot run forever. Sooner or later the world catches up with you.

For me it happened shortly after I turned seven. It was at First Night Ceremony. Oh, how excited I was to be going. The food, the singing, the fireworks—especially the food. It never occurred to me that my world would shift beneath me, that my life . . . But then, you know all that, or else you would not be here. In fact, you know much more, my young friend, than I did when I was in your place. It has taken me most of my life to convince the Pyong Myar that there was no point in keeping you as ignorant as they kept me.

Still, it is sweet to remember, even now—sweet and terrible to think of how we put on our

robes of yellow and crimson and made our way
through the streets with all the others. My family
went with our neighbors. Their daughter Shula
was my best friend, and she held my hand as we
wound through the streets.

We laughed together at the bloody clowns
along the way.

We were that innocent.

I still remember standing with the crowd at the
foot of the temple, looking up at each level. The
first seemed so much higher to me then—twice
man height, it was nearly four times my size.
How I loved to see the guards standing on it all in
a row, their weapons at the ready. Then, ten feet
behind it and twelve feet higher, the second level
with the costumed maidens in their robes and
scarlet feathers. Then the third level with the
priests, the fourth with the watchers, the fifth
where the Pyong Myar stood waiting.

The Pyong Myar. I see the cloud that passes
over your face. He is frightening, is he not? Do
the children still tell each other stories of what he
will do to them in the night if they are bad? I
feared him with that delicious fear of childhood
that made me want to hide when his name was
mentioned at the same time that I wanted,
hungered, to hear more about him.

This was the first time I had ever seen him. I
shivered happily at the sight, since I was clinging

to my mother's skirts and therefore believed myself to be safe.

The Pyong Myar stood at the top of the temple, surrounded by a ring of fire and holding two huge knives above his head as if he planned to carve a hole in the sky. The trumpets blared, the people shouted, and to my utter horror, the Pyong Myar began to walk down the great line of steps that runs up the center of the temple.

What was he doing?

A silence fell over the crowd. The watchers, the priests, the maidens, the guards became motionless.

The Pyong Myar continued his slow progress down the steps, ritually crossing and uncrossing his knives as he walked.

Shula whimpered next to me, and received a sharp rap on the head from her father's knuckles for the transgression.

The Pyong Myar was the tallest man I had ever seen, an effect that was heightened by his fantastic headgear. His crimson robe flowed behind him. Though he was well over a hundred and seventy-five years old, the muscles that shifted beneath the leather straps of his chest harness were those of a young man.

"What is he doing?" I whispered to my mother. "Why is he coming down here?"

This earned me the same treatment that Shula's whimpers had earned her,

The guards dropped to one knee when the Pyong Myar reached their level. My own knees began to buckle, and I must actually have started to drop, for my mother grabbed my shoulder.

The crowd was stiff and silent, and young as I was I could feel the tension among them. As the Pyong Myar began the descent from the first level of the temple to the ground a murmur of astonishment rose, then quickly died. The only sound in the entire city was the metallic hiss of the Pyong Myar's knives as the blades slid back and forth, back and forth, across each other's surface.

We were standing some fifteen feet from the front of the crowd. The Pyong Myar placed his knives together, upright, then spread them apart. At this gesture the crowd separated as smoothly as if some invisible blade had thrust among us, slicing us into two groups. We jostled back in eerie silence, leaving a path about five feet wide through which the Pyong Myar could pass. I stared across that space at Shula, who stood shivering next to her father.

The Pyong Myar began to walk down the aisle he had created, glancing from side to side. To my horror I realized that his eyes were blue, and glowing. I clung still closer to my mother as he approached, my fear so great I could hardly breathe. Once he had passed us by I nearly collapsed with relief.

But he had not gone more than eight paces past us when he turned and walked back to where we stood.

He stopped directly in front of me. I tried to back away, but there was no hole in the solid wall of flesh behind me, no nook or cranny into which I could escape.

He stared down at me. Awe-stricken, I gazed up at him.

He extended the knives, placing one on either side of my neck. "You!" he said. Then he drew the knives forward, slicing two lines—See? I have the scars still—along my jaw.

My mother shouted in triumph.

My father began to weep.

The Pyong Myar reached down and took my hand. His grip was utterly unlike anything I had ever felt before, and I did not even know the word for it until my third year in the temple when I was given some ice from the top of the mountain. His grip was *cold.*

My mother pushed me forward. The crowd was silent, save for Shula, who whispered, "Good-bye, Banang!" as the Pyong Myar led me away from my parents and my childhood, up the stairs of the temple.

I was hard put to keep up with the Pyong Myar, for the steps were too large for my childish legs. It was a terrifying climb. With no warning I had been pulled from the crowd by this fearsome stranger and taken from my family, who I was quite sure I would never see again. Something dark and mysterious had reached out and chosen me to be part of it; something that was only whispered about in the city. Yet such was the awe in which we held the temple ceremonies, and the power that emanated from the Pyong Myar, that I did not cry out, did not resist, only did as I was expected. I tried to do this with some dignity, but it was not easy when I could barely negotiate the steps, and I was crying out inside with loss and terror, as well as the pain of the cuts on my jaw.

The guards, already on their knees, bowed their heads to the ground as we crossed the broad terrace on which they stood. Despite my terror, part of me wondered if this display of respect was for the Pyong Myar, or for me. For little as I knew what was in store, I knew that children chosen in this fashion were considered rare and precious.

As we mounted the next level of steps, I turned to glance behind me. I could still see my parents in the crowd below. A fierce tug from the Pyong Myar brought me face forward again.

The maidens bowed in the same way the guards had, though I noticed at least one of them secretly glancing up to get a better look at me.

The priests, too, touched their heads to the ground as we passed. Only the watchers in their blue robes did not move but stared intently, as if burning my image into their brains.

At the top level of the temple, the level where the Pyong Myar had stood alone, he turned me to face the mob below. Carefully, almost tenderly, he set the huge knives on a stone table. Then he put his hands around my waist, which was wet with my own blood, and lifted me above his head.

The crowd roared its approval.

The Pyong Myar turned and carried me through a dark door.

As you know, it is ten strides from that door to the Pyong Myar's private apartments. Were you as astonished as I at the luxury of them? I had not known what to expect, but the lavish tapestries, pillows, rugs, fountains, polished woods, and silky curtains were a surprise.

My new master placed me upon a table, and though he did not tell me to stay, I knew better than to attempt to move.

It was a relief when he removed that terrifying headdress and I saw that beneath it he was only a man after all. A remarkable man, but a man nonetheless.

"Do you know why I have brought you here?" he asked.

I shook my head. I had some vague idea, but no certainty, and no voice with which to say so.

He smiled, which did nothing to make his face any less frightening. "Carna and Sangua spoke to me. 'We have sent the next Speaker,' they whispered in my mind. 'Go and find him, and train him, so that he may serve the people.'" He paused, and for an instant—I will never forget it, for I never saw it again—a look of weariness passed over his features, and they seemed to sag with age. "It has been too long since a Speaker appeared," he said. "I have been worried for the people. It is good that you are here."

I nodded, feeling a little bit better. I wanted to be good.

He looked at me, and I saw the second thing that I have never seen in him again. It was pity, and it terrified me.

"Do you know what the Speaker does?" he asked.

It took me a moment to answer, for my tongue seemed to be sealed to the roof of my mouth. "He has visions," I said at last. "Visions that guide the people."

"And do you know how he does it?" asked the Pyong Myar.

I shook my head, relieved to be able to answer without words.

He closed his eyes and sighed. But he said nothing more on the matter. A moment later two women came to the door, and I sensed that it was with some relief that he gave me into their care. They washed my wounds and smeared them with an ointment that burned like fire. Then they tucked me into a strange bed, and sang me to sleep with songs I had never heard before.

This was my entrance into the Red Temple.

My life in the temple soon fell into a pattern. The women who had taken me from the Pyong Myar's rooms, Lala and Ariki, became my guardians, and—more important—my teachers. They began by teaching me the history of our city, the stories of our wars and our victories, and the tales of our enemies, the terrible enemies that are always waiting, lurking, ready to overwhelm us. They told me stories of those who speak the language of blood, and how their words have ever and again saved us from surprise, helped us avert disaster, led us to salvation.

They told me that I was to be the next Speaker. But they did not tell me what that meant, nor how I was to make this transition. That knowledge was kept from me for the time being.

My only dissatisfaction was that I was kept within the temple walls, a prisoner in a golden cage. I did have other children to play with, children of the guards and the temple women. One, especially, became a friend. His name was

Mam, and he was Ariki's nephew, an arrogant scamp who somehow managed to sneak out of the temple and roam the city on a regular basis. Mam loved to tell me what was going on outside our walls, and after a time I begged him to look in on my family, and on my friend Shula.

He, in turn, tried to convince me to sneak out with him. The night I agreed to try we were caught, of course. He was severely beaten. I was not, and while my escape from punishment was a great relief, it also left me feeling extremely guilty.

Mam was far too much the scapegrace to hold this against me, but he no longer suggested that I accompany him on his adventures. It was clear to me that whoever ruled our lives did not care if Mam entered the city, and cared a great deal whether I even attempted such a thing.

The night before my eleventh birthday Lala took me aside and said, "Tomorrow you will be initiated into the next level of the temple. A man will come to take you away. Go bravely, and do not shame your second mothers, Lala and Ariki." She closed her eyes and drew me to her. "It is possible we will not see you again, my little one, my Banang," she whispered. The tremor in her voice frightened me, and I threw my arms around her and wept.

The next day the two women dressed me in my finest clothes. The rest of my things were packed in a wooden chest. Late in the afternoon the chest and my trembling self were set outside the doors of our apartments. Lala and Ariki each embraced me and told me to be good, wise, and brave. Then they closed the door. I could hear two things. The snick of the metal as they slipped the bolt and locked me out, and their cry of lamentation as they mourned my loss.

I stood and waited, trying to be brave.

It was not easy.

After a long time, or at least what seemed like a long time, the Pyong Myar came to me. I had not seen him since the night he delivered me to Lala and Ariki. He was naked, save for a black cloth tied around his waist and a red cape that flowed from his shoulders.

"Are you ready, Banang?" he asked. His terrible voice was gentle, almost worried.

When I nodded he reached down and took my hand. "Someone will come later to get your things," he said. Side by side we walked along the corridor. Because I had a feeling it might be a long time before I came here again, I stared hard at the images carved on the walls, the pictures of gods and heroes, trying to burn them into my mind.

We stopped before a carving of a tree. The Pyong Myar reached out with his free hand and pressed one of the fruits. To my surprise, a large section of the wall slid open, revealing another corridor beyond. I had walked past this hidden door hundreds of times without ever knowing it was there.

"You will learn many secrets before this day is over," said the Pyong Myar. "This is but the least of them."

The corridor was lit by oil lamps. Between them hung tapestries woven with pictures from the stories I had been taught by Lala and Ariki.

The Pyong Myar led me to a room that was as large and comfortable as his own. Yet it felt close and still. It took me a moment to realize that this was because it had no windows.

In the center of the room stood a table made of stone. The Pyong Myar told me to lie down upon it.

A moment later a slender, dark-eyed man entered the room. He was nearly as tall as the Pyong Myar. He looked young, except for his eyes, which seemed very, very old.

"This is Banang," said the Pyong Myar, gesturing to me. "Your successor."

The man smiled and nodded to me. "I have been waiting for you for a very long time," he said. He sounded weary, a little sad. I felt guilty, though I had no idea what I could have done to hurry things along.

As if he had read my mind, the man said, "Do

not worry, Banang. It is not your fault. The world turns as it will. Sometimes relief comes sooner, sometimes later. I still have years to wait. But knowing you are here and ready to begin makes my heart lighter."

I nodded, said nothing.

The man turned to the Pyong Myar. "Leave us," he said. "I will do what must be done."

To my astonishment, the Pyong Myar turned and left. I would not have believed that anyone could give him an order.

"My name is Naranda," said the man. "I am the one who speaks the language of blood. This is not an easy thing, but it must be done. I do it for the people. It is you who will do it when I am gone."

I stared at him, eyes wide, but said nothing. I am not sure I could have spoken had I wanted to.

"To do this, you must be prepared," continued Naranda. "That is why you are here today. What I do to you today, you will do to others later. Almost always you will take from them. Only once in all the years that follow will you give as I am about to give to you."

His eyes were powerful, his voice soothing. He was moving closer to me. As he spoke, his eyes began to change. Soon they were glowing, deep red, like coals in a firepit. Then he smiled, and I saw for the first time the sharp fangs that curved down from beneath his upper lip.

I wanted to scream, but found that I could not, could not move, could not resist.

Naranda bent over me. My heart was pounding so fast that I feared it would explode. Drawing back his lips, he plunged his fangs into my neck.

A spasm wracked my body. Fire seemed to pour into my veins.

Then the world disappeared and I found myself floating in a strange nothingness. Odd shapes, made of mist and edged with fire, whirled past me. Voices whispered in my ears.

I thought I was dying, but knew that I could not be that lucky. The agony was exquisite.

Then all went black.

When I woke, Naranda was sitting nearby. He looked tired, gray, worn-out. He raised his head, and the eyes that had glowed red when he first approached me now seemed empty, as if the fire had consumed what was there, and only cold ashes were left.

"You live," he whispered.

I nodded.

"I was afraid you might not." His voice sounded like dried corn husks rustling in the wind.

I wanted to rage at him for what he had done to me. But his weakness was like a poultice, drawing out the sting of my anger. Whatever his purpose, his action had clearly cost him as much, possibly more, than it had cost me.

"Are you all right?" I asked.

"I'll live. I have to, until you are mature yourself. Who else will speak the language of blood until then, if I do not? Can you stand?"

I tried, and found that I could—found, in fact, that I felt surprisingly strong.

"Help me up," said Naranda.

"What is the language of blood?" I asked, as I drew him to his feet.

"It is the language to which you were born, Banang," he answered. "It is words of warning, whispers of prophecy; tomorrow itself singing a song that only the drinkers of blood may hear and repeat, only the Pyong Myar interpret."

I did not understand, nor did he expect me to. At his command I led him to a pallet. It was covered by a finely woven robe. When he lay upon it I noticed, with a shudder of revulsion, the line of dried blood that ran from the side of his mouth. My blood. Looking more closely I saw that traces of it circled his lips as well. As if aware of what I was looking at, he flicked his tongue at the corners of his mouth, trying to clean away the brown flakes.

"Tell me what you have done to me," I said, my voice quavering.

"I have made you a man of the people," he

replied. "When I am gone, it is you who will read the secrets written in the language of blood."

I stared at him, saying nothing.

"When the time comes for your change, your body will grow in the ways that all young men's bodies do—with this addition. Like me, you will have the bloodteeth." And here he drew back his lips to show the fangs with which he had pierced my neck.

Ah—I notice you looking at me nervously. Do you want to see mine? Don't be shy; I don't mind. Here. Impressive, are they not? And never more so than when blood is in the offing.

Naranda became my teacher, and for the next three years I was trained in the ways of the Speaker. This was difficult, for at first I could not stand to be near him, as his very presence brought to mind our first meeting and what he had done to me. But after a time I grew used to him and even, I suppose, to love him. He taught me a great deal: how the Sources are chosen, and why they die after their third contribution; why those who speak the language of blood can never see the sun again; what it is to live longer than anyone save the Pyong Myar.

This and more he taught me, as I will teach you. He prepared me well to take his place, and when in the spring of my sixteenth year he finally died, I felt that I was ready. My own change had come upon me nearly two years earlier, and as my voice had deepened, my shoulders broadened, so, too, had my bloodteeth developed, just as Naranda promised.

He had prepared me for everything, except for what I found when I climbed the stairs to meet my first Source.

The stairs, as you will eventually see, are on the outside of the temple. They lead to a small structure on the very top of the building. The walls of this structure are chest high—tall enough to hide what happens within them. It has no roof save the sky, and the moon's light fills the chamber. Inside is a stone table, much like the one in this room.

An eager dread, a mix of excitement and terror, filled my heart as I climbed to the top of the temple. I had been moving toward this moment all my life. The breeze was cool. I could see the city below me and knew that the people depended on me, on the knowledge I would bring them. I wanted to be a good Speaker, yet feared the act that would make me one.

Fear turned to dread when I walked through the door and saw my Source waiting for me on the stone table.

It was Shula, of course. Not mere coincidence,

but the will of the Pyong Myar. This act would be the test and the binding of my will to speak the language of blood.

She was not bound. There were no guards. She could have walked away.

But she lay waiting for me.

"It has been a long time, Banang," she whispered, as I stared at her in shock and horror. "I have missed you."

"And I have missed you," I said at last.

I felt as if two snakes were fighting in my stomach, twisting and writhing. I was torn between the fire that was stirring in my blood and my horror at using my long-lost childhood friend as my Source.

"Why do you look at me that way?" she asked. "Are you angry?"

"Why are you here?" I replied.

"They chose me. I came. Just the same as you."

"Run away," I said, my voice flat, my heart filled with shame at the betrayal of the people carried in that simple sentence.

"Will you run away with me?"

I shook my head. She shrugged, as if to ask how I could possibly expect her to do what I would not.

I sat beside her on the stone table and we talked of old times, of our families, of what had happened in the years since I entered the temple. Too soon I saw in her eyes that the moon was overhead, and I could wait no longer. I stood, turned away, turned back. My mouth ached as the bloodteeth grew for the first time, stretching down past my upper lip. She closed her eyes, extinguishing the moon, as I bent over her and pierced the smooth flesh of her neck.

Her blood pumped into my mouth, hot and fragrant, and the gods reached down to touch me. Despite my revulsion, I drank deep, sucking the blood through the wounds I had made.

Then the Fit of Prophecy came upon me. As Shula's blood released what is in me, that part that makes me a Speaker began to read the secrets of the blood, the past of our people which flows in all our veins and points to our future. Fire crawled along my limbs. The heroes whispered their messages. Images swam before me, not like a dream but like a new reality, sharper and more clear than anything seen before. I was transformed, and my heart saw into the past and the future with eyes that would shame a hawk's.

I fell to the floor, writhing and jerking, as the words flowed out of me. The tiniest part of me was aware of the Pyong Myar standing nearby, taking down everything that I said.

When finally the fit ran its course, I slept as if I were dead. When I woke, I was in my own room.

The Pyong Myar was again nearby, staring at me. He smiled when I opened my eyes, and said, "You did well."

The sickness in me made it impossible to answer.

"It is always this way after the first time," he said. "You will feel better tomorrow."

What he did not know was that I suffered not merely the sickness of the First Speaking. I suffered a sickness of the heart, a terrible guilt and fear over what I had done to Shula.

He showed me what I had spoken, the words of blood that told the future of our people. It would be a good year, but a cloud was growing on the horizon, a darkness yet unclear. Thus was the importance of the speaking reinforced. Knowing that this danger was coming, we could begin to prepare. In six months I would again speak the language of blood. Perhaps then we would know what the danger was.

Shula and I were married, of course. My first bride. How many since, I have lost count. A year for each, wed at the first speaking, taken to new heights at the second, separated by death at the third.

Six months later a new bride.

I will be glad to lay the mantle down.

Naranda, I suspect, did not find this all so difficult. In the training he gave me, there was no hint of the pain that I felt in regard to Shula. For him, it was the way it was. Maybe he had forgotten. Maybe he had never cared.

I cared. I brooded day and night about Shula's fate.

The second speaking came and went. She was pale and weak for many days afterward. But the speaking had been important. A war was brewing, enemies gathering in the distance, forces joining against us. This we needed to know; this we would not have known, save for the language of blood.

I went to visit Lala and Ariki. I could not tell them what I was thinking, that I could not do this again, not when I knew that it would mean the death of my Source, my friend, my love. They knew what I was thinking anyway, of course. They always did. Without a word they let me know that my thoughts, my doubts, were shameful.

Finally I spoke to Shula. "We should run away," I said.

"Silly Banang," she answered. "What is, is. There is no running away."

But I persisted. Every night I whispered to her that we must leave the city, flee to the jungle.

"Silly Banang," she would respond. "You have tasted the blood. You must drink now, whether we are here or in the jungle."

"I can find other blood," I replied. "It does not have to be yours. I do not want you to die. We must leave, we must leave."

Then she would put her hands on either side of my face, resting her little fingers in the scars the Pyong Myar had made the night he took me from my family. Looking deep into my eyes she would ask, "Then who will speak for the people?"

For that, I had no answer.

"Silly Banang," she would whisper. Then she would cuddle against me, and lying in my arms fall asleep.

I could not.

I noticed the Pyong Myar watching me and wondered if he knew what I was thinking. He took me aside to talk to me.

"The next time you speak the language of blood will be terribly important," he said, his face stern, his blue eyes glowing with that horrible fire. "If all goes well, you will speak of the enemy and his plans—where the army gathers, when it will attack. This is what you were born for, Banang. You will tell the city what it must know in order to survive."

I did not tell him of the hollow horror growing in my heart. I could not make the words come past my thick, rebellious tongue.

The night before my third speaking, a year since I had first tasted Shula's blood, a sunrise and a sunset before I would be called upon to drink until she died, I said to her, "We are leaving the city."

The horror in her eyes matched what was growing in my heart. But its roots were different. She could not imagine this terrible act of betrayal. "What will the people do without us?" she asked.

"I don't care," I replied. My voice was savage. "I don't care about the people. I care about you."

She looked down. She did not answer. I knew she was ashamed for me, but that she would come with me if I insisted.

I insisted. Late that night we left the temple, slipping out through the secret ways that Mam had taught me long ago, the first and only time that I had ventured into the city after the night of my calling. I feared that we would be spotted. My plan was to run. Once I had been called the fastest boy in the city. I did not know how fast I was compared to the guards, but counted on love and fear to put wings on my heels. I knew that Shula could not keep up. But if I escaped myself, at least she would live. I did not want to lose her. But better to lose her yet know she still lived than to lose her to the demands of the language of blood.

Or so I thought at the time.

No one stopped us.

We traveled far from the city, deep into the jungle.

Two nights later we found the enemy.

It might seem like the oddest of chances. It was not chance. There are no coincidences. The heroes led me there, to see what I needed to see.

We came upon the army when we climbed a hill and saw, in the valley below us, row on row on row of tents, stretching as far as the nearly full moon could show us.

These men were coming to take the city. If they were successful, they would rape the women, kill the children, loot the Red Temple.

There were no words to be said. Language was not needed. Shula took my hand and turned me around. Silently, carefully, we made our way back to the city.

The Pyong Myar stood at the temple door, the not-quite-secret door through which we had fled, through which we returned. He did not speak, only nodded, his eyes dim and sorrowful.

The next night I climbed the temple stairs to the low-walled room where Shula lay waiting on the stone table. I swallowed the rest of her life, and as she lay dying I writhed on the floor and spoke again the language of blood. All the secrets of the past, all the wisdom of the people, all the strength of the heroes flowed from my tongue. In the language of blood I told not only the location of the enemy, which I well knew, but their numbers and their plans and their secret weaknesses.

The city was saved, of course.

I have had many Sources since then.

I am more weary than I can tell you.

I am glad you are here.

So. Now you know what it is all about, know far more than I did the day I came to Naranda.

Are you ready? Place yourself here, please.

Turn your head just so.

This will only take a moment.

Old Glory

Donald B. Henderson
Civic Responsibility Class
Ms. Barnan
Sept. 15, 2041

**Essay: The Day
I Did My Duty**

Y GREAT-GRANDFATHER
was the craziest man I
ever met. Sometimes
it was embarrassing even to have him be part of
the family.

For example: You should have seen how he
acted when Congress passed the S.O.S. law last
June.

He actually *turned off* the holo set!

"Well, that's the end of life as we know it," he
said as the image started to fade. Then he stared
at the floor and started to mutter.

"Oh, Arthur, don't be ridiculous," said my mother.

She switched the set back on and waited for the newsgeek to reappear in the center of the room.

"Ridiculous?" yelped Gran-Da. "You want to see ridiculous? I'll show you ridiculous!" He stood and pointed to the big flag that hangs over our holo set. "*That's* ridiculous! Thirteen stripes, sixty-two stars, and not a bit of meaning. After what they did today it's all gone."

"That's not so, Grampa," said my father quietly. His voice was low and soft, the way it gets when he's really angry. "Now sit down and be quiet."

That was a relief. After Gran-Da came to live with us I was always afraid he was going to get us into trouble. So I felt better whenever Dad made him be quiet. Sometimes I wished Dad would just throw him out. I didn't really want him sleeping on the streets, like all the old men I walk past on the way to school. But I didn't want to make our Uncle angry either.

Later that night, when I was going to bed, Gran-Da called me into his room.

"How you doing?" he asked.

I shrugged. "I'm okay."

Gran-Da smiled. "Are you afraid of me?"

I wanted to say no. Only that would have been a lie. So I just nodded my head.

"Afraid I'll talk dangerous?"

I nodded again. I didn't know what I would do if my friends were ever around when he started talking like he does sometimes. I knew what I *should* do, of course. But I didn't know if I could do it. I mean, he *was* my great-grandfather, even if he was crazy and wicked.

He looked sad. "Are all the kids at your school like you?" he asked.

"What do you mean?"

"Scared little sheep, afraid to talk."

"I'm not afraid to talk," I said loudly. "I just don't talk nonsense, like . . ."

I broke off.

"Like me?" he asked, scratching at the little fringe of white hair that circled the back of his head. (I don't know why he never got his head fixed. All the other great-grandfathers I know have full heads of hair, whatever color they want. Not mine.)

I looked away from him. Suddenly I realized what was wrong with his room. "Where's your flag?" I asked.

"I took it down."

I must have looked pretty funny. At least, the look on my face made him snort.

"How could you?" I asked in a whisper.

"It was easy," he said. "I just pulled out the tabs at the corners, and then—"

"Gran-Da!"

"Donald!" he replied. "When the government passed S.O.S., they took away the last thing that flag stood for. I don't want to look at it anymore."

He paused and stared at the floor for a while. I looked at the door, wondering if he would say anything if I just left.

Suddenly he looked up again. "Listen, Donald. I'm ninety years old. That's not that old, these days—I could probably last another thirty."

That was no news. It was one of the reasons my mother was so upset when he moved in. I felt sorry for her. Thirty years of Gran-Da was my idea of a real nightmare.

"The thing is," he continued, "I'm just a normal guy, not a hero. But sometimes there's something you have to do, no matter what it costs you."

I looked at him in horror. "You're not going to do anything crazy, are you?" I felt sick in my stomach. Didn't he understand he could get us *all* in trouble? If he wasn't careful, the Uncles might come and take us away. I glanced at the ceiling, half expecting it to open up so that a giant hand could reach down and snatch my great-grandfather then and there.

"Why are you telling me this?" I asked at last.

"Maybe I'm hoping that if I scare you enough, it will make you start to think." He shrugged. "Or maybe I just want to see what you'll do."

"Can I go now?"

"Yeah," he said bitterly. "Go on. Get out of here."

I slipped out of his room and ran down the hall to my own room. I flopped onto my bed and lay there, staring up at my beautiful flag and trembling.

I thought about Gran-Da all that night. I thought about him in school the next morning, while we were saying the pledge, and the Lord's Prayer, and reciting the names of the presidents. I remembered what Gran-Da had said the first time he heard me recite the list—that there had been more presidents than we were naming, that some of them were being left out.

I wanted to talk to my teacher, but I was afraid.

The next morning was Saturday. When Gran-Da came to breakfast he had a red band tied around his head. He was wearing a vest with fringe on it, a blue shirt, and faded blue pants; he was carrying a lumpy plastic bag. He had a button on his vest that looked like an upside-down Y with an extra stick coming out of it.

"What's that?" I asked, pointing to the button.

"A peace symbol," he said. He dropped the bag to the floor and settled into his chair.

"Really, Arthur," said my mother. "Don't you think this is carrying things a little too far?"

"S.O.S. was carrying things too far," said Gran-Da.

My father sighed. "Look, Grampa, it's not really a problem. If you don't break the rules, S.O.S. won't have any effect on you."

I was amazed to hear him say that. Then I decided he must be trying to get Gran-Da to calm down. It didn't work. Gran-Da shook his head stubbornly, and suddenly I knew what he had in the bag.

My throat got thick with fear. I couldn't finish my breakfast.

After breakfast I followed Gran-Da out of the house. He was heading for the town square. I was pretty sure I knew what he was planning. My stomach was churning. What if the Uncles thought he had polluted our whole family?

I could only think of one way to save us. I slipped into a televid booth to call my Uncle. When I told him what was happening he looked stern and shocked.

"You won't hold this against the rest of us, will you?" I asked nervously.

He shook his head. "Of course not," he said. "You've done the right thing. We'll have to come and talk to all of you when this is over, of course. But I wouldn't worry about it much."

The screen went blank. I hurried back out to the street.

I felt embarrassed, and frightened. But I was also a little excited. Would the S.O.S. men really show up? My friends would think I was a real hero. I hurried toward the town square.

Gran-Da was already there. He had climbed onto the bandstand, of all places, and he was shouting about S.O.S.

People looked at him nervously. To my surprise, a few actually stopped to listen. I stood beneath a large tree, about a hundred feet away. I didn't want to get too close.

Suddenly Gran-Da reached into the bag and pulled out the flag he had taken off his wall the night before. Holding the upper edge, he rolled it over the side of the bandstand. A slight breeze made the stripes slide and shift.

I covered my face with my hands and wished the terrible scene would end.

Where were the S.O.S. men?

"Friends!" cried Gran-Da. "When I was a boy this piece of cloth used to stand for something. Yes, it did. In fact, it stood for a whole lot of things. Ideas. Like that a man should be free to say what he thinks, and worship where he wants, and get together with other folks if it pleases him."

More people were stopping to listen now. Someone started to boo.

"But that's all over!" shouted Gran-Da. "Bit by bit, piece by piece, we've given away all the things this used to stand for. S.O.S. was the end of it. Now this poor old flag doesn't stand for anything at all.

"That being so, I think it's time I put it out of its misery."

I looked around. Where were the S.O.S. men? Why didn't they get here?

Now that people realized what Gran-Da was going to do, they started to back away. Some of them left. I could tell that others wanted to, wanted to get as far away from the terrible thing he was about to do as they possibly could. But they couldn't bring themselves to go. They wanted to see if he would really do it.

Gran-Da raised the flag and lit a match.

"Good-bye, Old Glory," he said sadly. "It was a good idea while it lasted."

He touched the corner of the flag with the match. Nothing happened, of course, since like all flags it was made of flameproof material. You can't burn a flag even if you try.

Gran-Da knew that. He wasn't stupid—just

crazy. A crazy, dangerous person—the kind who could ruin the wonderful country we've built.

Suddenly I saw the S.O.S. men. They looked beautiful in their blue pants, white shirts, and red vests.

Gran-Da saw them, too. I know he did.

So it's not like it's my fault, really. He had a chance. Everyone knows that even though the new law allows for instant executions, the Shoot-On-Sight men are supposed to give a guy a chance.

But Gran-Da didn't care. When his first match went out he lit another one. He held it to the corner of the fireproof flag and just stood there, smiling at the three men.

So everyone could see that he was crazy.

The men lifted their laser rifles. The leader counted to three, and they fired in unison.

The light sliced right through the old man. He toppled over the edge of the bandstand. The flag curled around him as he fell. He was still holding it when he hit the ground.

My throat got thick. I could feel tears at the corners of my eyes. Crazy, I know. But he was my great-grandfather, after all. So I don't think it was too bad to feel a *little* sad about what had happened.

That doesn't mean I don't know I did the right thing by calling the S.O.S. guys. I mean, think about it. What would happen if other people started to believe like Gran-Da—crazy things, like that everybody should be allowed to say whatever they wanted to?

What kind of a world would that be?

The Passing of the Pack

THE CAVE WAS DARK. Even so, I could see well enough to know when the wolf lurched to his feet and began walking toward me. I pushed myself backward, until the cave wall stopped me. The wolf continued to advance. His eyes, locked on mine, were like the kind of coals you find late at night: nearly spent, yet still holding the power to burn—or to kindle a new flame.

I thought of red-haired Wandis, safe in some distant village, and wondered if I could somehow change my mind. But of course it was far too late for that.

The wolf lowered his head, then curled his black lips in a snarl, revealing yellow fangs that glistened with saliva. I held my breath to keep from crying out in fear.

Dying-ember eyes still locked with mine, the beast moved closer. My self-control was weakening. But before I could disgrace myself with a scream, his teeth sank into my flesh, and I fainted.

How long I lay on the floor of the cave I have no idea. It could have been an hour; it might have been days.

When I finally woke I felt drained of strength. Even opening my eyes seemed more than I could manage. Wondering if I had been a fool (or perhaps more accurately, just how much of a fool I had been) I began to review the strange events that had led me to this moment, starting with my first encounter with the great wolf.

It had happened eleven years earlier, when our little village was being battered by the worst winter in memory. I was only five at the time, but I knew it was the worst because my grandmother told me so. She seemed to take most of her pleasure from telling me how much better or worse or bigger or smaller everything had been when she was young, so if she said the howling winds and driving snow that lasted for weeks on end were the most ferocious she had ever experienced, I felt it must be true.

It must have been bad for the wolves, too, for they had never troubled us before then. But one night, when thick snow was dropping like wet feathers onto our already snow-choked village, they came, slipping through the dark as silently as whispers between friends. Their killing was quiet, too, until the warm blood emboldened them, and the village animals took fright. Then the silence was broken by a growing commotion.

I was among the first to hear it, possibly because my sleep had already been disturbed by strange dreams that night. I didn't understand what was going on, of course. I only knew something had roused our small flock of chickens.

Even at five I was trying to fill in for the lack of a man in our house. So when I climbed down the ladder from the little loft where I had my bed, I moved as soundlessly as possible, hoping not to rouse my mother from her sleep. I slipped into my coat and pulled on the fur-lined boots my grandmother had made for me. Then I pulled open the bottom half of our door. But the way out was blocked by drifted snow. I closed the bottom of the door and opened the top. Then I fetched my stool and clambered through the opening.

I almost disappeared in the snow. Sputtering and cold, I dug my way out of the drift. Fortunately, the snow was not that deep everywhere. The same winds that had blown it against our door had cleared other places almost down to the hard-packed paths we had made over the last two months. Wading over to one of the paths, I headed for the henhouse.

After a few moments I sensed a dark form on my left. A moment later I realized there were two more on my right. A sudden fear clutched my heart. I would have turned back, but the house seemed suddenly very far away. Moreover, I had a favorite hen, a biddy with golden feathers, that I loved too dearly to lose. In my childish mind, I somehow thought I could protect her.

Or perhaps I thought that she would protect me.

Anyway, as I struggled my way to the small henhouse the surrounding commotion grew louder. I knew it would not be long before other folk came out to tend their livestock, too.

Once inside I gathered my hen in my arms. As I was trying to soothe her a dark form surged through the doorway. The light was too dim for me to see it clearly, but I had no doubt that it was a wolf. The hen squawked and struggled in my arms. It was hard to say which was beating more frantically, the hen's wings or my heart.

The wolf growled—a low, throaty sound that

moved me to a new level of fear. It stalked forward. Clutching the hen as if she could protect me from the beast, I watched the wolf draw nearer, until I could smell its hot breath.

Suddenly another, larger wolf leaped into the henhouse. It hurtled forward and slammed against the first wolf. After a moment of growling and scuffling one wolf slunk away. The second wolf stepped forward. I knew it was the second because its outline, which was all I could see, was so much larger than that of the first wolf. It took my hen from my arms and closed its jaws. The bird was dead.

The wolf nudged me with its head, then turned and trotted from the coop. Overwhelmed by its presence, I started to follow it, completely forgetting the first wolf. But it had not forgotten me; it moved in front of the door, refusing to let me pass.

The wolf kept me prisoner for only a few moments. But it was time enough for the village to finish rousing. Soon the streets were filled with shouts and screams. Then, above it all, I heard a howl that seemed to pierce my skull and shiver down my spine. I believe it was a signal of some sort, for the wolf that had been guarding me turned and ran from the coop, leaving me alone with a flock of hysterical chickens.

My mother found me soon after that. Torn between rejoicing that I was safe and wanting to beat me for my foolishness, she bundled me in her arms and carried me back inside. Then she began to cry. I felt very bad. I thought: *If I had a father, he could have taken care of this trouble.*

It was three summers before I saw another wolf. I had lost my way in the forest and was just beginning to panic when one of the creatures stepped from behind a tree. I jumped in alarm, but it simply sat and gazed at me. When it was clear that my panic had passed, the wolf came and took my sleeve between its teeth. Its grip firm but gentle, it began tugging at my arm. As it seemed to have no inclination to harm me, I followed it—though the truth is I probably didn't have much choice anyway. Before long it had led me to a familiar clearing, where I saw a village girl named Wandis gathering flowers.

I paused before stepping into the clearing. When I looked down the wolf had vanished. Pretending that I had intended to come this way all along, I stepped into the clearing. Wandis and I walked home together.

Though she was a year or so younger than I, Wandis and I became friends. Her companionship was a comfort to me, for it was not easy to be fatherless in our village, where I was often taunted as "No man's son." I blamed my mother for this, though later I began to see that it was as hard for her to raise me without benefit of a man as it was for me to grow up that way. Yet whenever I asked her about my father, she became vague and avoided answering my questions directly. This was hard, for I longed to know who had sired me.

A few times during these years I would wake in the night at some noise below me, and peering through the cracks in my floor I would see a tall, dark-haired man sitting at our table. Once he was holding my mother's hand. Another time he was kissing her.

I wanted to kill him. I wanted him to come live with us. I was angry at him for only coming at night, when I was in bed and could not get to know him.

I wanted him to love me.

My mother died when I was ten, and I did not see the man again. I went to stay with my grandparents.

About the time of my fifteenth birthday I began to see the wolves more often. Sometimes when I woke in the night I would draw open my window and spot one of them sitting beside the house, staring up at me. Or if I was walking home from a late visit with one of my few friends, I might hear a sound and turn to see a wolf behind me. Once spotted, it would sit and stare until I turned and went on. They never chased me, never made a move against me. But neither would they let me approach them. Whenever I tried they would bare their fangs and raise their hackles.

I did not mention them to anyone, for our village was a superstitious place. But in the end my silence was of little value; the villagers turned against me anyway.

Of all the people in the village Wandis was my closest friend. I thought her very beautiful, with her red hair and strangely blue eyes. Yet she was as much an outcast as I, somehow unable to fit properly into the life of the community. Naturally, this gave us something in common.

Sometimes when I went to the forest to gather wood, or simply to be alone, I would find Wandis on her hands and knees, examining some plant. She knew wonderful things about them. Once she showed me a small, low-growing vine called Sal-o-My-Heart; it was adorned with clusters of miniature red berries, and she claimed it could be used to make a man or woman fall in love. I asked her to give me some, teasing that I might use it on her. But she only blushed and turned my attention elsewhere.

I remember that day well, because a few weeks later one of the village women accused Wandis of witchcraft. She said Wandis had used her powers to steal her husband's love. I thought it more likely the woman's own nagging had turned her husband away, and his eyes had strayed to Wandis because she was young and very lovely. Even so, I asked Wandis if what the woman said was true. She patted my cheek, and told me not to be silly.

It was not so easy to turn aside the village elders. She could not pat *their* cheeks and tell them to go away when they came to take her. When I spoke out on her behalf, I was accused, too. ("Only a witch would defend a witch," they said.)

We were given a trial, which was a mockery, and sentenced to be burned at the stake. And this they would have done, had not the wolves come to our rescue.

It was late October. I was bound with stout ropes and thrown into a woodshed built against the side of one of the elders' homes. The space was cold and cramped, and though a little light filtered in during the daytime, after sunset it became completely black. Yet my thoughts were less of my current discomfort than of the morning, and the flame. I wondered how long it would it hurt. I wondered, too, how my fellow villagers could be so cruel.

Shortly after midnight I heard something scratching outside the wall of my prison. I felt a shiver run down my spine, for I had no idea what it was, and there were many tales in our village of the strange things that wander after dark.

The noise went on for some time. It seemed to be getting closer. Then it stopped. Suddenly a great, furry shape was pressing against me. Had I not become so used to the wolves I might have died of fright right then.

The wolf began to gnaw at the ropes that held my hands and feet. It was not long before they parted under his sharp teeth. Taking the leg of my trouser in those same teeth, he guided me to the wall, where I discovered the hole he had dug to get in. It took some work to enlarge the hole enough for me to wriggle through it. By the time we were done, I was hot and sweaty and filthy. But I was also free!

The wolf whined and tugged at my trouser leg again. Obviously he wanted to get away from the village as quickly as possible. But I would not go until we had freed Wandis, too.

As it turned out, the wolves were ahead of me. A familiar voice whispered to me from nearby. Only the soft growl of warning from the wolf at my side kept me from crying out her name. I moved forward to embrace her, but two huge wolves stepped between us, barring my way.

"Don't be foolish!" I hissed angrily.

They bared their fangs. The sound that rumbled in their throats was too soft to wake those sleeping in the house. Nevertheless, the menace it contained was genuine.

The wolf that freed me had been joined by another of the beasts. They tugged at my clothing again, even as the ones beside Wandis started to pull her away from me. She looked back once as they led her into the darkness. That was my last sight of her, for the wolves beside me began herding me, just as insistently, in the opposite direction.

It was a clear night. The sky was drunk with stars and a half-moon hung low on the horizon, silvering the trees, the village, the wolves. It was darker when we entered the forest, and I had to concentrate to keep from stumbling over the great tree roots that erupted from the ground at odd intervals. I bumbled and crashed along, but the wolves seemed to make no sound at all.

Finally we came to a small cave. The wolves led me inside, then settled themselves in front of the entrance. Obviously, I was supposed to stay here. It seemed I had only traded one prison for another.

But why?

I was kept in the cave for two weeks, guarded by the pair of wolves that had brought me there.

As soon as I saw them in the daylight I was able to tell them apart. One had a wild eye, blue and strange, that seemed to look into another world. The other was marked by a ragged ear, which I assumed had been earned in some youthful battle.

Several other wolves came to the area during this time. Usually they brought small game for me to eat, though sometimes I got the feeling they were coming simply to look me over. I felt that I was on display.

Wild Eye and Ragged Ear escorted me to a nearby stream whenever I wanted to drink. Once, convinced that they would not hurt me, I tried to run away. But they set up a howling, and before long the woods around me were thick with wolves. I was herded back to my cave like a lamb being herded by a shepherd.

The mystery finally ended on All Hallows' Eve, when Wild Eye woke me from a sound sleep by nudging at my face.

"What do you want?" I asked crankily.

He took my arm and pulled on it.

"For heaven's sakes," I said. "It's the middle of the night!"

This didn't seem to make any difference. Realizing I wouldn't get any sleep anyway, I decided it was easiest just to follow him. Ragged Ear joined us at the entrance to the cave. Walking on either side of me, the two wolves led me deeper into the forest.

It was an eerie journey. The bright moon cast a glow over the trees that made the woodland seem entirely different than during the day. A cool breeze rustled through the leaves, heavy with the rich scent of the forest. To our left I could hear a tiny brook tinkling its way over polished stones. The silent wolves pressed against my legs.

After a time we came to another cave. A dark-haired man sat in front of it—the same man I had seen kissing my mother so many years ago. He was lean, and though there were deep lines in his face, I could see that he had once been very handsome. On closer inspection I noticed that the hair that had seemed so black was shot through with silver. His eyes were deep set, and dark as the night.

Wild Eye and Ragged Ear moved to his side.

The man stood and embraced me. "Welcome," he said. "I am glad to see you, my son."

How could I respond to this? I was glad, for my heart had reached out to this man even in those brief glimpses of him that I had had so long ago. But I also felt great anger that he had not been with me while I was growing up. I wanted to hit him. I wanted him to hold me. I wanted to say all that, but didn't know how.

"Where were you?" I whispered at last.

"Here," he said. "Where I belong."

"You belonged with us," I answered.

He shook his head sadly. "No man can do all the things he ought," he said. He returned to his seat. The wolves stayed at his side. "It is always choices," he said, resting a hand on Wild Eye's head. "I doubt any man is ever sure he has made the right one. But once you have made it, you have to live by it."

He said these last words fiercely, as if he thought them very important.

"This was your choice?" I asked. "To live in the forest instead of with your family?"

"To be where I was most needed," he answered.

"I don't understand," I said.

"You will," he whispered. "Soon enough, you will."

Other wolves were gathering around the edge of the area where we sat. Their yellow-green eyes gleamed at me out of the night. A cub, small and fuzzy, came to nip at my father's foot. He poked the cub with his toe, and it rolled over to have its belly scratched. My father obliged, but only briefly. The cub's mother came and picked it up by the scruff of its neck, then carried it back to the circle that was forming around us.

"What do they want?" I asked, somewhat nervously.

"They are here to pay homage," said my father.

My puzzlement must have showed in my face. "I am their leader," he added, as if that explained everything.

I swallowed. "How can *you* be their leader?" I asked.

He smiled, a sad, wise kind of smile. "You know the answer," he said, "but you have tried to pretend that you were wrong. Now the time for games, for hiding, is over. Now you have to examine the truth."

A terrible thought had struck me when I first saw him sitting there. I had pushed it firmly aside. Now my father was forcing me to let it come forward again.

"You're one of them!" I whispered.

He nodded serenely. "I am one of them."

I stumbled over the questions that sprang into my mind. "I don't understand," I said at last.

"They need me," he said simply. "The pack always needs a man to keep it together, to make difficult decisions when times are hard."

I remembered the winter when the wolves invaded our town. "That was you in the henhouse!" I accused.

He nodded.

"Why did you kill my chicken?" I cried, remembering my childish grief and feeling doubly betrayed that it was my own father who had caused it.

129

He laughed, a short bark that bordered on contempt. "You sound as though you have never eaten a chicken yourself," he said.

He was right, of course, and I blushed at my question. Yet he went on to answer it.

"I protected you," he said. "As I tried to protect everyone in the village." He sighed. "I brought the pack only because we were starving. Afterward, I wondered if it had been a mistake. I do not know. As for your hen—I thought you might as well learn early on that you were going to have to give up things you loved for the wolves."

Something in his words disturbed me. "What do you mean, give up things for the wolves?"

He leaned against Ragged Ear. Suddenly he looked old, and tired. "My time is almost up," he said. "The pack will need a new leader soon."

I recoiled from him in horror. "You want *me* to become a werewolf!" I cried.

He nodded. His dark eyes were locked on mine.

I was appalled. My own father was asking me to become one of the creatures of the night our priest had warned us about.

"It's evil!" I hissed.

My father's eyes flashed dangerously. "I am not evil," he snapped. "I made a choice a long time ago, a choice I have lived by, and honored—which is more than most men do. If that does not fit your little priest's petty idea of morality, it is no concern of mine." He spat on the ground in front of him, dismissing the priest. "You know you do not belong in that village. Do you want to try to become like them? Or do you have the courage to reach for your true destiny?"

I pressed my hands against my head, as if that could keep out these frightening thoughts. It was true. I wasn't like the others. I had always known I didn't really belong there.

But did I belong here?

I looked at the pack that had assembled around us. *These are my father's people,* I thought. *They love him. He fits here. He . . . belongs.*

I remembered how it hurt to know I was not truly a part of my village, to feel that invisible wall against me. I wanted to belong, too. I wanted to fit in as he did.

But was this the place?

"Tell me more about it," I whispered at last.

He gave me a wolfish grin.

Hours later I sat in front of my cave, hoping the morning sun might somehow dissipate the chill that seemed to have settled into my soul. My father and I had talked long into the night. I understood better now how much he had given up to become the leader of the pack, and what he had gained. I understood, too, what I must give up to follow his path.

My shape was the first thing. If I agreed to his request, I would become a man only five times a year: on All Hallow's Eve, and on the nights of the solstices and the equinoxes. These were the nights my father had slipped into the village to visit my mother. It occurred to me that she must have loved him very much, to be so lonely for him.

My human shape was not the only price.

"I am young, for a man," my father had told me. "But my body has aged as though it were a wolf's. My time is short. I must pass the burden soon, or the pack will be left without a leader."

"And if I refuse?" I had asked.

He had shrugged and looked away, the only sign of his agitation the way his fingers worked in the scalp of the wolf he had been stroking. "I cannot force you."

But he could entice me. And he did, talking of the joy he felt when he ran through the forest with the pack at his side, and the richness he found in their community. Yet he did not hide the darker side of their life, and he told me, too, what it was like to catch a smaller animal and kill it in your jaws, and feel its warm blood trickling down your throat.

But mostly he spoke of the wolves and his deep

love for them. He cared for them as if they were his children, making decisions, settling squabbles, keeping the pack away from the world of men where they would be hunted and killed.

I could tell he had been a good leader, wiser and far more compassionate than the village elders who had sentenced Wandis and me to death.

It was to be our only talk. He would not assume his human shape again for another month and a half, when the winter solstice came. And, one way or another, he would be dead before then.

I picked up a stick and threw it at Wild Eye, who was sitting several feet away. He blinked at me, as if he thought it an astonishing thing to do. But he didn't move. I hated him, hated all of them, for taking my father away from me. His life had been shortened by his wolfhood. Now he was like a candle whose wick was guttering in the last bits of wax. Even worse, he had made it clear that the effort of passing his power, which was what he wanted more than anything else in the world, would make this the last thing he would ever do. If I accepted it, he would die in giving it to me.

I thought of Wandis, led to some distant village by the wolves. Did she wonder what had become of me? What if I did this thing, and then came to her as a man on the first night of winter, to tell her what I had become? Would she still care for me? Would she wait for me, as my mother had waited for my father? Or would she draw away with the same horror that I was still trying to fight down in myself?

I looked at my hands and tried to imagine them as paws.

I shivered, and stood up.

At once Wild Eye and Ragged Ear were at my side.

"Not supposed to let me go anywhere, are you?" I asked.

They stared at me.

I wondered what it would be like to be able to talk to them as my father could. I realized he was part of a whole world I was unaware of, a mysterious world of night and secrets. I was curious about it. I wished I could run with the pack for a night before I made my decision.

Another wolf came limping along the path. Though it was the first time I had seen him in this shape since I was five, I knew it was my father.

He made a motion with his head that I took as a command, then turned and headed back down the path. I rose to follow him. My guards made no move to stop me. When we had gone a way, my father dropped back to walk beside me. I looked at him and shivered. It was strange to see that dark, four-legged shape and know my father was inside it. And stranger still to think of inhabiting such a shape myself.

Passing through the quiet forest, we came at last to a rocky hillside where nearly two dozen wolves were gathered. Some were playing. Others lay dozing in the warm morning. Now and then their legs would twitch, and I knew that they were running in their sleep.

After a while I thought I understood why my father had brought me here. These were his people, the responsibility he wanted to pass on to me. He stepped into the clearing, and the others were instantly alert. I could sense their love for him. He came back and took my hand softly between his jaws, then drew me in beside him. He was introducing me.

The wolves crowded around us. I felt myself overwhelmed by their warmth, their musky odor.

"All right," I whispered. "I'll do it."

I opened my eyes. My father's naked body lay beside me, quiet and empty, but human once again.

I was still human, too.

Half relieved, half disappointed, I began to wonder if something had gone wrong. Then the moon slipped over the horizon and began pouring fire into my veins.

I cried out in agony. For all we had talked, my

father had not warned me of the terror of the transformation, not spoken of the fear and the pain that strike as your skin begins to stretch, your bones wrench themselves into new shapes, and your teeth curve into deadly fangs.

I fell to the ground, writhing in pain.

And yet even in my pain, part of me watched in fascination as thick tufts of hair sprouted on my hands, my fingers curled into paws, and my nails thickened into strong, black claws. I began to rip at the clothing that seemed to bind me like a rope, shredding it in my torment.

As abruptly as it began, the change was complete. I stood on all fours, trembling with the wonder and the horror of what I had just experienced. Then I tipped back my head. Staring at the moon, I howled for the loss of my father, whom I had never had a chance to love.

Almost instantly Wild Eye and Ragged Ear detached themselves from the darkness and came to stand at my shoulders.

"Run with us," said Wild Eye, and I was not surprised when I understood him. "Run with us. It is good for sorrow."

I stretched my legs and headed into the night with them, and then stopped, almost dizzy with sensation. It was as if I had been blind and suddenly found that I could see. Except it was not only my eyes that were keener now, but my nose and my ears as well. I could hear the voles rustling in the soil beneath me, and smell where the weasel had passed an hour before. Stranger still was finding a man-scent and then recognizing it as my own, the path I had followed the day before. What a shock, to discover I had possessed such a rich and distinctive odor, and been so unaware of it.

But the biggest surprise was yet to come, as one by one the pack reached out to greet me.

"Welcome!" cried each voice in my head. "Welcome, welcome, and thrice welcome!"

How can I write of this thing that my father could not tell me, of this oneness that we share? For each of them is always with me now. And the pack is more than a pack, it is a being of its own, of which we are all a part. As they took me in and embraced me as their leader, I knew why my father had loved them so.

I knew, too, that I had found my community at last.

I am a wolf, and I will never be alone again.

Tonight is the night of the winter solstice. I have spent my precious time as a man writing all this down, while it is still fresh within me. When I have finished, I will also write a letter to Wandis. Because it is too soon for me to leave the pack, I will ask Wild Eye to carry it to her, tied around his neck.

But three months from now I will travel myself

to the village where the wolves took her. And on the night of the equinox, when the change has come over me and I am a man once more, I will go to her, to learn her answer.

I think if anyone can accept this, it will be she.

I hope I am right.

After all, someday I too will need a son to whom I can pass the pack.

A Blaze of Glory

T WAS A HOUSE full of white bread and death. Silence grew beneath the chairs like balls of dust. Nothing was out of order, nothing seemed to breathe.

In the center of it sat an old woman, waiting to die.

That she had been full of life at one time I well knew, for she was my grandmother, and I had seen her eyes flash with a fire that seemed stolen from the stars; heard her laugh in the night with a clear joy that easily banished my terror when I was upstairs, lonely and moon-frightened.

Now that was gone, the fire and the clarity drowned in the muddy depths of an unyielding old age that, glacierlike, had crept across her and locked her in a grip of ice. Loss lay like dust in every room of the house: loss of husband; loss of friends; loss of strength, of sharpness of sight, keenness of ear, delicacy of touch. Loss, most of all, of memories, the most recent going first, so that if I entered the house and greeted her, then went to the kitchen to make her some tea, she would cry out in surprise when I re-entered the room five minutes later.

If I reminded her that she had said hello to me minutes earlier, she would shake her head, moaning that she was worthless.

Even that was not as painful as when she asked where my grandfather was, and I would have to remind her that he had died three years earlier. She could only remember him alive, and only knew he was dead when it was brought to her attention. Every day, sometimes more than once a day, she learned again that the man she had lived with for over fifty years was gone, endlessly repeating that horrible first moment of discovery.

Her memories peeled away like layers of an onion, each layer with the power to bring tears to the eye. I found myself growing younger in her eyes as she remembered me not as her youngest and most disgraceful grandchild, the high-school dropout with no prospects, but as the little boy I used to be. I wondered if her failing mind would finally carry her to a time before I was born, and if so, if she would then forget who I was and no longer recognize me when I came to visit.

This had been going on for some months before I began to suspect that as she lost memories she might not be simply moving away from the present, but might indeed be moving toward something else, something long lost that she wanted to regain.

"I can almost see it, Tommy," she moaned once, holding my hand, her eyes squeezed shut, something like tears but thicker oozing from their corners. "What was it? What *was* it?"

But the memory, and then the thought, eluded her.

By the next week she was confined to her bed. Being the only one in the family without a job, I began to visit daily to care for her.

It was during this time that she began to hint at her secret. "Did you ever see them?" she asked one afternoon while I was sitting beside her bed, working a crossword puzzle.

"See who, Gramma?"

"The fair ones," she replied impatiently, as if I

were a stupid child not paying attention to something obvious.

"I don't think so," I said cautiously.

She sighed, then whispered, "Of course not." After a moment she added, "I wish you had."

"What are you talking about, Gran?" I asked, totally mystified.

She closed her eyes. Her face relaxed, and for a moment I thought she had fallen asleep. But when she spoke I realized that she was seeing something in her mind.

"Elves," she said. "I'm talking about the elves."

"I wish I had seen them," I answered with some conviction. I had the terrible feeling that she was finally losing her mind. Even so, it was a fact that I had wanted to meet an elf from the first time I had read about them.

"I helped them once, you know," she continued. "At least, I think I did. Do you think I helped them?"

"Of course," I said, squeezing her hand. It was the first note of whimsy I could remember hearing from her in many years, and I was amused. Amused, and oddly touched. I found something both sweet and very sad in the way we were exchanging roles, me becoming the grown-up, she the child.

"Didn't I ever tell you about it?" she asked. Before I could answer, she muttered, "Oh, of course not. I'm not supposed to talk about it. Never did, either, till now."

It was one of those moments she had when she suddenly seemed to lurch into the present.

"You can tell me about it," I said.

"Probably shouldn't," she muttered. Then she did sleep.

The next day she seemed stronger and more alert, and for a moment I wondered if her body was actually growing younger along with her mind. But the look in her eyes was almost feverish.

"I'm so glad you're here," she said. "I want to tell you about them. I think it will be all right."

It took me a moment to realize that she was talking about the elves again.

"I was nineteen," she said, leaning toward me and whispering, even though there was no one else in the room. "And only recently married to your grampa. Falling through was an accident, actually, but they were desperate, and I was able to help them."

"How did you meet them?" I asked. I felt myself slipping easily back into a childhood mode where I had listened eagerly to her stories. Besides, there was no harm in humoring her.

"I fell through," she said softly. "I was walking

across the field, the one between the house and the barn. One minute I was there, the next . . . *pfffft!*" She made a burring noise, almost a raspberry. It was quite funny, coming from that ancient, wrinkled face.

"Where did it happen?" I asked. "Where, specifically?"

"You know," she said slyly.

"The fairy circle?"

She nodded.

I felt a slight shiver. In the field between the house and the barn was a perfect circle about fifteen feet in diameter where the grass never grew quite right. My sister and I had always called it the fairy circle and said it was where the elves came to dance. I had had a lurking fear of the spot from the time I was in fifth grade and had bought a book of "strange but true" stories from our school book club. One story in particular had terrified me, a tale about a man who had vanished in full view of his wife and children while walking across a field. He was never seen again, but his children once heard his voice emanating from the exact spot where he had disappeared, calling faintly for help. Afterward, the grass around that place had never again grown quite the way it should.

The story and the "fairy circle" in my grandparents' field had merged in my mind, and I had usually given the spot a wide berth. Being of scientific mind, I had decided that the disappearing man had fallen into another dimension of some sort. Despite our name for it, I had never thought of our "fairy circle" as actually belonging to magical creatures. It was simply a place to watch out for. Now my grandmother's words were making me reconsider that position.

I shook my head and smiled at myself. What foolishness! I was being drawn in by her senile fantasies. But what harm in it? It seemed to make her feel better to tell the story. It certainly wouldn't hurt me to listen.

"What happened after you 'fell through'?" I asked.

Gramma closed her eyes and didn't answer for a long time. "So beautiful," she whispered at last. "So beautiful—and so sad."

"What was so beautiful?"

"The elves. Their world. I wish you could have seen it, sweetheart. It was more wonderful than I can tell you. But someone was dying." She paused, then added ruefully, "Like me."

I wanted to tell her she wasn't, but she had never appreciated that kind of comforting dishonesty. So I simply said, "Tell me more."

She sat up. It startled me, for she had not been able to do so on her own for several days. But it was as if the story she wanted to tell had overtaken her, was holding her in its grip.

"I was afraid when I first fell through," she said, her voice husky but strong. "Thank goodness I had read *Alice in Wonderland.* I don't know what would have happened to me if I hadn't. I think every child should read *Alice,* don't you, Tommy? It doesn't make any sense, but neither does the real world. It's a very educational book."

She shook her head. "Listen to me babble. I don't have much time; I have to stop going on so. Listen carefully. Otherwise you will forget. You can't count on memory. Memory can betray you." She paused, drew a breath, then said, "All right, here's what happened."

I listened carefully. That night, I wrote down what she said:

When I fell into the land of the elves, I was afraid; terrified. Not so Dyor, the elf who found me. He was tall, Tommy, tall and terribly beautiful—so beautiful that it made me ashamed to be seen by him. I felt like a little brown wren next to a magnificent cardinal.

I didn't see him right away, only the world into which I had fallen. The field was like our field, save that there were no fences or barns, the grass was somehow more lush, the flowers brighter, the sky more wildly blue. A sweet breeze blew through the grass.

Floating on the breeze was an enormous lavender butterfly; it landed on my shoulder, as if it could not imagine being afraid of me.

Then Dyor stood, rising from the grass like a dream. He had been sleeping, he told me later, and my arrival had woken him.

"Thank the seventh star you are here," he said.

It's hard to tell you what his voice was like, Tommy, except to say that it wasn't simply beautiful; it was *thrilling.*

He must have seen that I was trembling. Or maybe he simply realized how I would feel. Anyway, he raised his hands, palms out, and said, "Please do not be afraid. We have been hoping someone would come. We need your help."

When I asked him what he meant, he shook his head and said, "Let me show you. It will be easier than trying to explain."

Taking my hand, he led me out of the field and into the woods. Such woods! Such *trees!* I felt that our trees were copied from them by some third-rate manufacturer.

Dyor led me to a grove filled with elves. They blinked and turned away when they saw me, as if something about me hurt their eyes. It made me sad.

At the far side of the grove stood two

thrones, carved from burnished wood that had a strange grain. Sitting on the thrones were two elves, one male, one female. He was the most exquisite of all the elves, with silver hair that seemed to hold its own light. She should have been beautiful, but was not. Something had happened to her, weakened her somehow, so that she seemed to be wasting away.

The elf king stood and held out his hand to me. I crossed the grove. I was shaking. Not because I was afraid he would do anything to me, but simply because he was so wonderful. It was like meeting a god. At the same time, I was fretting inside over how I would ever get home to your grandfather. Of course, he wasn't your grandfather, yet; we had been married for less than six months at the time. But I knew I had to get home to him.

When I reached the elf king I knelt before him and bent my head to the ground. I had never met royalty before, but I had read my books, and it seemed like the right thing to do. After a moment he reached down and put his hand under my chin. His skin was warm and smooth. "Stand," he said in a voice even more wonderful than Dyor's.

I stood.

"What is your name?"

"Ivy," I said, hoping he wouldn't think it too foolish.

I was pleased when he smiled. "A beautiful name," he said. "For a beautiful young woman."

I began to blush. I knew I could not be beautiful in their eyes, but it pleased me that he said it.

He stared at me for a long moment, squinting a bit as he did, as if I hurt his eyes. "We need your help," he said at last. Even though Dyor had said the same thing, I found it astonishing. What could these people possibly need from me?

I started to say, "I will do anything I can," then stopped myself. These people were magical, after all. Who knew what they might ask of me? I wanted to help, but I didn't want to commit myself to something that would keep me from going home again. Choosing my words more carefully, I said, "How can someone like me help someone like you?"

The queen stirred then, moving as if it hurt to do so. "This is my fault," she said. "It is best that I explain."

Her voice sounded not like bells but like sand running between your fingers, and it was all I could do to make out her words.

The king paused, then nodded. I was aware of the elves all around me, staring at me. The queen held out her hand. I took it, wondering if I should kiss it, wishing Dyor would advise me. But the queen simply squeezed my fingers, then pulled her hand back. Unlike the king's, her hand was cool, almost cold.

"I have made a serious error," she said softly.

The king was frowning.

I waited, but no one spoke. Finally I said, "What did you do?"

"I stayed too long at the fair."

I didn't know what to say to that, so I just stood and looked at her, waiting for her to go on.

"The goblin fair," she said at last.

The king looked away.

"There are rules," said the queen. "It is never wise to ignore them."

She straightened herself in her chair. I remember that specifically, because it was hard for me to imagine that someone so graceful could ever be uncomfortable. Finally she went on:

"Once a year the peoples of faerie gather at the goblin fair. It is a time of guaranteed peace, when dwarf and elf, goblin and sprite can freely meet and mingle, trade and talk, exchange everything from newts to news. I love the fair, love it too much, I suppose, for last year I broke the rules and stayed past midnight. When that happened, when I made that fool's mistake, the goblins took, as was their right, their penalty."

She closed her eyes and looked away.

"What was it?" I asked. "What was the penalty?"

"A part of me," she whispered. "They took a part of me and wrapped it in a stone, and now the stone is warm, but I am cold, and I am fading, and in time I simply will not be, unless the stone can be recovered."

I shivered at what she told me.

"It is part of the stone's enchantment that no elf can touch it," she continued, "nor no magical creature of any sort. Only a human can hold the stone. Would you do that for me, go and fetch the stone, bring it back so that I can be whole again?"

It would have taken a heart far harder than mine to say no to that, Tommy, though I did worry what your grandfather would say when I got home.

Well, getting that stone took longer than any of us imagined. What an adventure I had getting it back to the queen! Dyor and I met stranger creatures and saw wilder places than I can tell you about—giants and unicorns, and once I even saw a cave where a dragon lived, though I didn't see the dragon itself.

But with Dyor's help I did it, Tommy. We found the stone and carried it back to the queen. And when we did, when I placed it in the queen's hand, the most amazing thing happened. It was as if the stone dissolved, melted right into her palm. Something seemed to change and grow in her then, so that she was suddenly—oh, right somehow. Healthy again. Herself.

My grandmother began to cough at that point, as if the effort of telling the story had caught up with her all at once. "No more today, Tommy," she said. "I'm too tired."

To my shame, I tried to get her to tell me more, even though I could see that she was exhausted. Of course I realized the story was quite mad. But I was also enchanted by it.

The next day she went into the hospital.

I visited her daily. She told me more about the elf world when she could, though mostly she was too weak. A single strand ran through all the memories. "I have to get home," she muttered as she wandered through the back corridors of her mind. "I have to get home."

For three days I thought she was speaking about coming back from her adventure. It was almost too late when I realized that she meant she needed to go back to the farm.

"I have to go, Tommy," she cried, late one night, clutching my arm with a strength that astonished me. "Take me home!"

I wish I were stronger. I wish bureaucrats could be slain like dragons. But this was not an elven adventure, and I was not able to free her from the hospital.

She freed herself, I think. Through sheer effort of will she made herself well enough that they let her go home, on the condition that someone stayed with her around the clock.

That was all right. I had nothing else to do.

Three nights later I knew she was going to die. A trip back to the hospital might have squeezed out a few more days, but they were days that she didn't want, and that would have been spent in a place she hated.

She wanted to be home.

It was about three o'clock in the morning when the elves arrived.

I was sitting in my grandmother's room, holding her withered hand, wondering which labored breath would be her last. Suddenly I heard a rattling in her chest. Her hand tightened on mine.

"It's time, Tommy," she moaned.

Then the wall on the far side of the bed turned to liquid silver, and the elves stepped through.

There were eight of them. The first, I was quite sure, was Dyor. The king and the queen came last. I understood what my grandmother had said, about feeling like a wren next to a cardinal. The fact that all the elves blinked and averted their eyes, as if my plainness was painful to them, added to the feeling. I wanted to crawl under the bed and hide from their beauty, wanted to shake my grandmother and shout, "They're here!" But I could not, couldn't move at all. It was as though time had stopped, frozen at the moment of their arrival.

Dyor reached down and gently separated my grandmother's hand from mine. "Hello, Ivy," he whispered, and when she smiled I knew that she was still alive.

In that moment I felt a shift, as if I had moved from the place where time had stopped to their place, where time went on in its own way.

"We are here to redeem a promise," one of the elves said to me as they began to cluster around her bed.

"What promise?" I asked.

"A long time ago your grandmother did me a great service," said the queen, whose voice was not like sand now, but like breeze through leaves, like birdsong in spring, like rain on a window late at night. "In return, we offered her a chance to stay in Elfland, where she would have been immortal. She refused."

The king took the queen's hand. "It was not that she didn't want to stay," he said. "She did. But she had made other promises."

I thought of my grandfather, and wondered if the old man ever knew what Gramma had given up for him.

"I offered her many things," said the queen. "But she had only one request. 'Let me be buried in Elfland,' she said to me, just before we sent her home. 'When it is all over, let me come back here to rest.'"

"So we have come to take her home," said the king.

Two of the elves were carrying a length of cloth, the color of the sky at midnight. Working gently, deftly, they slid it under my grandmother's frail body. She shifted slightly as they did, but was silent. I thought I saw a faint smile play over her lips.

Now the elves lined up, three to each side of her bed. Each took hold of the edge of the cloth. Together they lifted her from the bed.

Suddenly the liquid silver of the wall began to shift. It grew transparent, and I caught a heart-stopping glimpse of the world on the other side.

The king shifted his eyes so that he was looking right at me. He was squinting and frowning. It felt bad to be looked at that way.

"Would you like to see the Lady Ivy as we see her?" he asked.

"I don't know what you mean."

"You think we find you ugly, do you not?"

When I lowered my head in shame, the king laughed. "We see different things, you and I. Your senses observe the outside. Ours perceive what lies inside. Let me show you."

And so saying, he laid his hands upon my eyes. When he took them away I cried out in wonder. The elves were as beautiful as ever. But my grandmother—oh, my grandmother. What a blaze of glory she was.

Now I understood why the elves had averted their eyes.

Singing a song that broke my heart, they carried my grandmother through the silver portal, a small sun resting on the dark elven cloth.

"Your lives are short, Tommy," said the Elven king. "But, oh, how the best of you shine."

He reached for his queen's hand. Both of them nodded to me, then turned and followed my grandmother's funeral procession, through the shimmering silver portal, back to the land of the elves.

The wall closed behind them. I stared at it for a long time, then turned, and began to straighten my grandmother's bed.

A Note from the Author

FOR YEARS I have been maintaining that I can't really write short stories, that they are just something that happen to me by accident every now and then.

For an equal number of years Jane Yolen has been thumping me on the head (metaphorically speaking) and telling me that this is nonsense.

As usual, Jane was right.

It started with "The Box." Every once in a while a writer is given a gift—a bit of unearned grace. That is how I think of this story, which, of all the things I have written, is probably my personal favorite. In fact, it is my own feeling that it may well be the best thing I will ever write.

At one time that realization bothered me, particularly because it was written while I was still in my twenties. It was done, in fact, as an assignment for a class in children's writing that I was taking from picture-book writer Helen Buckley, who simply put a wooden box on the table one evening during class and told us to write a story about it.

Though I no longer remember exactly how the story grew, I do remember that I was certain it was the best thing I had written to that point. However, as is often the case with our best work, it was not easy to find a home for this story. After several rejections I consigned it to my files, where it remained for years, until Jane called and told me she was assembling a collection of short fantasies and wanted me to send her something for it.

With considerable trepidation, I dusted off "The Box" and mailed it Janeward. Three days later she called and said (and I have never forgotten this), "Bruce, this story is so beautiful that if the rest of the committee doesn't want it, I'm going to resign from the project."

Though I had already sold several books, that was the first time I knew I could write short stories.

Not that doing so then became a natural thing

for me. In fact, over two-thirds of this collection is a direct result of Jane personally prying stories out of my perpetually protesting psyche.

The usual cycle goes like this: Jane calls and tells me that she is doing a new collection and wants a short story from me.

I reply that short stories are an unnatural form for me and only happen by occasional accident.

She then tells me that this is nonsense, and that if I know what is good for me, I'll write a short story for her.

I reply that I will think about it.

If she noodges me enough times in the months that follow, a short story almost always results.

This has been a source of ongoing astonishment to me.

These stories happened in a wide variety of ways. "Old Glory," for example, was written out of sheer rage, my response to watching self-serving politicians prepare to sacrifice the First Amendment for a little short-term gain.

"Duffy's Jacket," on the other hand, was pure joy. The idea came to me while I was walking in the woods with some friends. When we got back to the house I excused myself, went upstairs, and typed it in a single sitting, the words seeming to fly from my fingers.

(If only it were always that easy! But I figure a

quarter century of word-wrangling entitles you to at least one story that comes fairly quickly.)

Speed was hardly the hallmark of "With His Head Tucked Underneath His Arm," which took nearly fifteen years to go from first draft to finished version (and then only got there because Jane and her brilliant assistant, Michael Stearns, helped me find an ending for the thing).

One thing the stories *do* have in common is that many of them were written in the middle of the night, a time I seem to find particularly fruitful for short stories. Both "The Passing of the Pack" and "Homeward Bound" (two stories that deal with my favorite theme of reconciliation) happened when I climbed out of bed and wrote them in the predawn hours.

Finally, again prodded by Jane, I began to realize that I had enough of these tales to make a collection. However, when I gathered them together and sent them to her, her response (gleeful and slightly sadistic) was, "I'll publish them as a book if you write some new ones."

Yikes! Torn between my conviction that short stories were something I write only when luck and the stars are with me, and my desire to see these all in one book, I swallowed my doubts and said yes.

And then put off writing them for nearly a year.

Unlike the other stories in this book, which were written months and years apart, the three newest ones—"The Language of Blood," "A Blaze of Glory," and "Clean as a Whistle"—grew simultaneously; often I found myself moving from the dark intensity of the vampire story to the sheer silliness of the brownie story in a single hour.

As always, no matter how bizarre the topic, in the end the main source of the writing is my own life and experiences and dreams. Thus "Blaze" is a tribute to my grandmothers, two of the most splendid women I have ever known, while "Blood" reflects some of my feelings about the act of writing itself. (As for "Whistle," I refuse to say what aspect of my life is represented, on the grounds that to do so could get me in a great deal of trouble.)

Oddly enough, when I was finished writing the last three stories, I found that I had finished something else as well. I had finally learned to believe in myself as a short-story writer.

So I hope you enjoyed yourself. Because I can tell you now, there's more where these came from!

About the Author

BRUCE COVILLE was born in Syracuse, New York. He grew up in a rural area north of the city, around the corner from his grandparents' dairy farm. In the years before he was able to make his living full-time as a writer, Bruce was, among other things, a gravedigger, a toymaker, a magazine editor, and a door-to-door salesman. He loves reading, musical theater, and being outdoors.

In addition to more than fifty books for young readers, Bruce has written poems, plays, short stories, newspaper articles, thousands of letters, and several years' worth of journal entries.

He lives in a brick house in Syracuse with his wife, his youngest child, three cats, and a dog named Thor.

Some of Bruce's best-known books are *My Teacher Is an Alien; Goblins in the Castle;* and *Aliens Ate My Homework.*